Sniff out other books by Victoria J. Coe

🚒 **Fenway and Hattie**

🚒 **Fenway and Hattie
and the Evil Bunny Gang**

Fenway and Hattie Up to New Tricks

Victoria J. Coe

G. P. PUTNAM'S SONS

G. P. PUTNAM'S SONS
an imprint of Penguin Random House LLC
375 Hudson Street, New York, NY 10014

Library of Congress Cataloging-in-Publication Data is available upon request.

Printed in the United States of America.
ISBN 9781524737832
1 3 5 7 9 10 8 6 4 2

Design by Ryan Thomann and Dave Kopka.
Text set in Chaparral.

For Kipper—
the Worst Patient Ever

CHAPTER 1

I scramble through Hattie's blankets, searching for the used-to-be bear. His legs are long gone. But he's still got an arm and a head with two button eyes. And most important of all, he's always here when I need him—just like Hattie. They're both always up for a loving snuggle or a thrilling game of keep-away.

Which I am about to win.

My expert nose leads me under the pillow . . . *chomp!* Game on!

I leap off the bed and tear around the room. Hattie's hot on my tail, waving a towel. She is the best short human ever, even if she's no match for a Jack Russell Terrier like me.

"Fenway!" she cries.

Ha! I dive behind the chair, my sides barely heaving. There's no way she can get me!

Hattie's bushy head appears. Her face is splattered with the wonderful mud we romped through on our walk. "Fenn-waay," she coaxes, her voice too sweet to be real.

Like I'd fall for that act. She's out to win!

Well, so am I, Hattie!

Her fingers brush my leg, but I'm already on the move. I shoot out onto the rug. I'm headed for the door when—

Whoa! Everything goes black. And there's a towel over my head.

Really, Hattie? Is this the best you've got?

One wiggle, two shakes, and the drape-y towel falls to the floor. Whoopee! I'm free again!

For the moment. I spin around, ready to take off, but find myself nose-to-nose with Hattie. And pinned between her legs.

Her eyes widen in victory. I gaze up at my short human's dirt-smudged face, so happy, so full of love. She's won. I've lost. Game over.

The used-to-be bear falls to the floor. There's only one thing left to do.

I leap into Hattie's outstretched arms. If the game's got to end, it might as well be on my terms. I sigh happily into her wonderful scent of mint and vanilla. And dirt.

"Aw, Fenway," she coos, nuzzling my neck. She sets me on the rug and rubs the towel over my mud-caked fur.

Aaaaah, that's the spot! I roll onto my back, my hind leg kicking with delight.

Hattie wipes my brown paw, then my white paw. A Long Time Ago, I convinced her that towel rubs are way better than baths. For us both! All it took was some kicking and thrashing—and maybe a lot of splashing, too. But what can I say? She learned her lesson well.

Hattie's still toweling me off when Food Lady's voice booms up the stairs.

"Uh-oh." Hattie glances at her own mud-splattered legs. She grabs the dirty towel and rushes into the hall. I follow her as far as the Bathtub Room.

"Uh-oh" is right! From the safety of the doorway, I hear water whooshing into the sink. Pretty soon, white soapy lather coats Hattie's hands and face. Her knees, too.

I wince. Even from here, I can smell her great muddy scent washing away. Then the odor of perfume-y flowers hits my nose. Eeeee-yew! And worse than that, Hattie's got an evil gleam in her eye. And a pile of suds in her hand.

My ears droop with worry. She's not getting any ideas, is she?

Hattie bends over. She purses her lips like she's about to blow those yucky suds at me. "Fenn-waay . . . oh, Fenn-waay," she taunts.

I step back, my hackles raised in alarm. "Oh no, you don't!"

Hattie busts into a fit of giggles. She blows the suds harmlessly into the sink.

I drop down in grateful relief. Of course, it was just a trick. Hattie's always looking out for me. How could I expect anything else?

Food Lady's voice booms up the stairs again. Hattie quickly dries her face and hands and knees. She looks me over, then dashes back to her room.

I spring up and trot after her.

Even though it's not bedtime, she grabs my hairbrush. She scoops me up and hastily brushes my matted fur. "Best buddies, best buddies," she sings.

I croon along, howling my own version of our special song. "Best buddies, best buddies," I yowl.

I climb onto her shoulder as she gives my coat a few last strokes. I'm so content, it takes me a moment to pick up a strange sound drifting in from the window.

Chip-chip-chip!

My ears perk up. I peer into the Dog Park below, searching for signs of trouble.

No squirrel-y intruders scurrying along the fence.

No trespassers clattering up the giant tree in the back or poking their rodent-y faces out of Hattie's little house up in the leafy branches.

The grass is calm and quiet, too. The ball Fetch Man threw for me after lunch is right where I left it. The Friend Gate that leads to the Dog Park next door is shut tight. And Food Lady's vegetable patch is as lush and tangle-y as it was this morning.

I scan the bushes on the other side of the Dog Park. My ears prick up. Even from way up here, I can detect rustling and humming. And wait—what's that? Something dives under a low branch. A little tail?

I try to get a better look, but right then Hattie decides it's time to go. She hurries over to the dresser and sets the brush on top. I shoot out of her arms, chasing her into the hall.

We fly down the stairs toward the smell of hamburgers. Hooray! Hooray! I love hamburgers! My dripping tongue can already taste them.

In the Eating Place, Fetch Man and Food Lady are at the table in their usual spots. I perch beside Hattie's chair, sniffing the delicious hamburger and ear of corn on her plate.

As soon as Hattie sits down, Fetch Man clears his throat. As he speaks, I catch a couple of words that I know—"Nana" and "here."

Nana? Here? My tail swishes with excitement. I love Nana!

Nana's the lady human who came and played with us. Back when we lived in our apartment way up high above the honking cars and snorting buses. She slept with me and Hattie when Fetch Man and Food Lady were gone.

Nana!

I can still taste the yummy treats she gave me. I can see her chasing me in the Dog Park. I can hear her cooing at me in her kind voice.

Ah, Nana! Is she coming again?

Maybe so. Fetch Man says "Nana" a lot of times, his voice energetic and eager, like he can't wait to go outside and play fetch.

Food Lady speaks in a happy voice, too. But she also sounds bossy, like there's a big job to do.

Hattie smiles and nods. She looks happy. But she smells worried.

And she's hardly touching her scrumptious food. Something is wrong. Hattie loves Nana as much as I do. What is she worried about?

As soon as I've munched my yummy kibble and the dishes start clanking in the sink, Hattie heads back upstairs. I'm right on her heels.

When we get to her room, she glances over her

shoulder. She lets out a breath, like she's relieved nobody's there. Is she glad nobody's playing chase with us?

Hattie quietly closes the door. She puts her fingers to her lips, shooting me a look of warning.

Whoa. Something important is about to happen!

I follow her to the closet, where she sinks onto the floor. She rummages through shoes and boots and toys. Reaching way in the back, she digs out a big box and wheels it into the room. She gazes at it, frozen. "Hattie-the-Grrate," she whispers.

I cock my head. I've heard those words before. Only they didn't sound miserable when Nana said them. In Nana's voice, they sounded exciting.

Hattie stares at the box with wide eyes, like it's a bone she dug up. But she doesn't smell happy.

My tail rises with curiosity. My nose gets busy sniffing. That box's scent is awfully interesting. And familiar somehow. Is Hattie worried about what's inside this box?

@HapteR 2

Cross-legged on the floor, Hattie stares at the box while I give it a thorough sniffing. Its scents are old and new at the same time. And also like metal and plastic. It's a cube, at least twice as tall as me, with wheels on the bottom. The sides are black, and the edges are shiny and metallic. The lid has hinges on one end and a buckle on the other. It's not like any box I've ever met. Talk about intriguing!

What was this box doing in the back of Hattie's closet? And more importantly, what is it?

Hattie's face scrunches. She doesn't seem to know what to do with this box.

So why'd she take it out of the closet?

I can't stand the suspense. I leap into her lap. "Great

news, Hattie!" I bark. "That box could have something wonderful inside. Like sausages! Let's open it!"

"Shhh," she says, frowning, like opening the box is the last thing she wants to do. But she clearly wants me to be happy, because she fiddles with the buckle and lifts the lid—*creeeak!*

My tail thumps with anticipation. I stretch way up, pawing the box, my nose sniffing feverishly. The smells are tantalizing! I need to see what's inside!

I spring onto the chair and peer down into the box. Wowee! My eyes don't know where to look first.

Hattie starts rummaging through silky cloth . . . a tall hat . . . a bunch of fake flowers . . . and she's not acting the least bit surprised. This stuff must be what she was expecting to find.

Hattie digs deeper and pulls out a flow-y cape, a skinny black stick, and a clear plastic box with a rattle-y ball inside.

I fly off the chair to investigate the growing pile of stuff on the floor. Everything smells new, like toys that haven't been played with. Yet at the same time, their aroma is awfully familiar.

The scents take me back to a lovely memory. Nana at our apartment with a box like this one. Nana in the flow-y cape, tapping the tall hat with the stick. Nana's fist, holding fake flowers.

Every sniff reminds me of that wonderful time. Hattie gaping in astonishment. Hattie clapping and cheering. Hattie clinging to Nana's side, full of admiration.

And best of all, I remember me and Nana playing tug-of-war with those silky scarves!

Sniff . . . sniff . . . licorice, coffee, just the right amount of cherry—*Nana!* This box smells like Nana!

It's definitely the same one she brought. Why didn't she take it when she left? And why haven't we seen it until now?

Hattie continues emptying the box, tossing metal rings and silky scarves onto the floor. My nose can hardly keep up with all the amazing things to smell.

Hattie waves the skinny stick through the air. She gazes at it, her eyes wide and full of wonder. It doesn't look like a stick from the ground. I scamper over for a better sniff.

But as soon as I get close, Hattie whisks it out of my reach. She plucks a scarf off the floor and stuffs one end into her fist, the rest of it snaking across the floor.

My tail twirls with excitement. I want that stick, but who can resist a game of tug-of-war? Especially with a silky scarf that's long and oh-so-bitable!

Chomp! My teeth sink into one end of the scarf. I dig in my hind legs and pull, tugging with all my might . . .

And whoa! I skid and stumble backward, crashing

into the chair. The scarf flies out of Hattie's hand, puddling in front of me.

"FEN-way!" Hattie frowns, waggling the stick. "Drop it!"

I unclench my jaws, my end of the scarf falling to the floor. It's pretty clear why she's unhappy. That game of tug-of-war was no fun at all. But only because she didn't even try.

She grabs the scarf, then shoots me a stern look. "Wait," she commands.

I plop down on my bum, tilting my head expectantly. She probably wants to play another game. I sure hope treats are involved!

Hattie makes another fist and once again starts stuffing the scarf inside her hand. She pokes and pokes until it completely disappears. "Watch," she says, tapping her fist with the stick.

An invitation if ever I saw one! I romp onto her knee, my jaws ready to nab that stick.

"Ab-ra-ca—no!" Hattie shouts. "Fenway, stay!" She waves it out of my reach.

"No fair!" I back into her arm, and the silky scarf slides out of her hand. Aha! I sink my teeth into it, but before I can take off, Hattie grabs me by the collar.

"FEN-way," she scolds.

I let the scarf drop. "What's the matter?" I bark. "Don't you want to play?"

She picks up the slobbery scarf, her eyes bulging as she studies tiny rips in the fabric. With a loud sigh, she hangs her head and tosses the stick onto the floor. "Hattie-the-Grrate," she mutters, sounding miserable.

I nuzzle against her leg. "Don't worry, Hattie. We can play some other game."

She lifts me into a hug. What can I say? Hattie's always up for snuggling—hey!

Plop! Suddenly, I'm inside the Nana-box. *Thud!* The lid shuts and I'm plunged into blackness. And trapped!

I paw furiously at the box. "What's the meaning of this?" I yelp. I jump as high as I can, but the lid won't budge.

I fall back down. Yikes! This box is dark and lonely. And scary. Clearly, the Nana-box is no place for a dog. I have to escape!

"Hattie, help!" I whine. "I'm stuck and I can't get out!" Isn't Hattie right outside the box? Why isn't she rescuing me?

She would help if she could. Maybe she can't hear me. I bark louder. "Get me out of here!" I'm about to try leaping again, when I hear a curious sound. I cock my head and concentrate.

"Shhhhh!"

Is that Hattie? Who is she shushing? It couldn't be me. I'm the one she needs to hear!

Tap! Tap! Tap!

I listen some more.

"Ab-ra-ca-dab-ra!"

Hattie's voice! She *is* right outside. I knew she'd come save me! "Hattie, it's me! Help! I'm in the box!" I scratch with all my might.

Snap! The buckle opens. *Creeeak!* The lid lifts up. Whew! It worked! She finally heard me!

I leap into her loving arms. The best place to be!

Panting with wild relief, I slobber her cheeks. "Thank you . . . Hattie . . . I knew you'd . . . come through!"

"Aw, Fenway," she sighs, patting my head. Clearly, she feels bad for my suffering. More than anything else, she wants me to be happy.

As the sky gets dark, we climb into bed. I go to wrap my paw around the used-to-be bear when I notice something curious. One of his button eyes has vanished. What could've happened to it?

CHapteR 3

The next morning, me and Hattie are out back in the Dog Park. After I scare away a couple of nasty squirrels, I rush over to her. She squints up into the hot sun and wipes her forehead. She smells worried again, which is no wonder after that terrible game we played last night. Being hidden and trapped in a dark, scary box is not any fun at all.

Good thing Hattie has me to remind her of better games to play! I romp over to the ball Fetch Man threw for us yesterday. "Let's play chase, Hattie!" I bark. I seize the ball and tear across the grass. She can't resist.

Or maybe she can. After rounding the giant tree near the back fence, I turn and stop. Hattie's plunked down on the porch steps, her chin in her hands. She looks defeated, and she hasn't even started to play.

She probably wants to be chased first. Well, I can change that!

I race through the grass to give her the ball, my sides heaving. I'm almost there when my ears pick up a horrible sound.

Chip-chip-chip!

I halt in my tracks. Intruder alert!

Hattie needs cheering up, but my other duty is calling. I drop the ball.

My fur bristling, I survey the Dog Park. Nothing appears out of the ordinary. All's quiet in Food Lady's vegetable patch. Or is it?

The low mesh-y fence wobbles. Out shoots a stripe-y chipmunk. His tail's straight out and swagger-y, like he's not totally trespassing where he doesn't belong.

The little villain scampers into the grass happy as can be. I spring into action. "Beat it, chipmunk!" I bark, rushing straight at him. "Or else!"

Chip-chip-chip!

He picks up speed, zigging and zagging, as if he actually has a chance of outmaneuvering the Master of the Dog Park. Well, he can try, but he won't succeed!

And really, he's making my job too easy. He may be fast, but he's got no technique. He heads right for the bushes, where I can pin him against the side fence lickety-split. Then it's game over, rodent!

Sure enough, he dives under the lowest bushy branch. I plunge in after him, ready to claim victory!

But where did he go?

The horrible chipmunk odor is everywhere. But he's not.

I root around under the bush, but he's nowhere to be seen. Did he just disappear?

I crawl through the dirt, the brush scratching my coat. He's got to be somewhere, right? But then again, chipmunks are always scurrying and then vanishing—*poof!* This guy could be three Dog Parks over by now.

I shimmy back out into the grass, where I hear jingling sounds. They're coming through the fence near the vegetable patch. Wowee, it's the ladies!

I hurry over and peer through the slats. A Golden Retriever and a white dog with black patches are rolling around in the grass next door.

I press my nose into a gap in the fence. "'Sup, ladies?" I call. I'm expecting to smell my best friends, Goldie and Patches. But their scents are different. I hope it's really them.

The dog I hope is Patches glances up and trots over. "Fenway!" The lovely voice sounds like Patches. The confident gait looks like Patches. But where did her smell go? "We were just talking about you," she says.

I cock my head. "You were?"

The dog who looks exactly like Goldie lopes toward me. "Well, *I* wasn't," she corrects in a very Goldie-like, growly tone. "My sister here was wondering what happened to you after our mud romp yesterday."

"What do you mean?" I ask. "Nothing happened to me. Did something happen to you?"

"You could say that!" Goldie huffs.

Patches turns to her. "That bath wasn't so bad."

Goldie harrumphs. "Are you saying you enjoyed the perfume-y shampoo? The too-cold water? The slippery tub?"

Patches sighs. "Aren't you being a bit dramatic?"

I shake my head. No wonder the ladies smell different. "Are you saying you had a bath?"

Goldie's eyes widen in surprise. "Are you saying you didn't?"

"No—I mean, yes. Hattie doesn't even try those anymore. Not since I showed her how much better I like cozy towel rubs," I say. "You should give that a shot."

Goldie raises an eyebrow. "Well, we didn't really have a choice."

"We went to a place." Patches shows off her claws, which are way smoother and shorter than usual. "It was quite nice, actually."

"If you like listening to protests. And sounds of panic," Goldie says. "Or smelling flowery soap."

"Now, Goldie," Patches says, her lovely voice bordering on irritation. "Don't give Fenway the wrong idea."

Goldie tilts her head. "*I'm* giving him the wrong idea? You make going to the groomer sound like a frolic in the park. Why don't you tell him about those nail clippers?"

Patches gives her a scolding look. "Goldie . . ."

Unbelievable! The ladies went to a place where dogs get shampooed? And have their nails clipped? "But your humans, didn't they try to save you?" I say, my fur prickling.

"Of course not," Goldie gruffs. "They handed us over, then just walked out!"

I quake with terror. This "groomer" sounds almost as bad as the vet who grabs and pokes and pricks. "Tell me you're making this up."

Patches gazes at me with eyes full of kindness. "It

wasn't nearly as scary as my dear sister remembers," she says, her voice soft and soothing. "Someday you'll find out for yourself."

"No way! Hattie always takes care of me," I say. "She would never give me a bad surprise like that." But as soon as the words leave my mouth, I remember getting trapped in that box and I'm not so sure.

CHAPTER 4

I'm still chatting with the ladies when I spy Hattie heading to the door. After a quick good-bye to my friends, I sprint after my short human. Something is probably wrong, and it's up to me to find out.

I stick by Hattie's side as she tromps into the Eating Place. The only tidbit I uncover is a stale but tasty corn-flake under a cabinet.

Hattie's pouring a glass of milk when the door to the garage opens. My ears shoot up. Somebody's coming! I rush over, my tail raised in alarm.

Fetch Man strides in, whistling. He's got a long pole in one hand. His arm's wrapped around a paper bag. A big can swings at his side.

I throw myself at his legs. "I'm so glad you're back," I bark. "I missed you so much."

He tries to pat me but apparently changes his mind. "Down, boy." He breezes into the Eating Place and dumps his loot on the table.

Food Lady comes in from the hallway. With a wide smile, Fetch Man hands her the big can. He unwraps a spongy roller and puts it on top of the long pole.

Food Lady pats the can, a deep look of satisfaction on her face. My tail swishes. It must be something wonderful. A giant can of chicken soup? Tomato sauce? Dog food?

I leap and leap, sniffing wildly, but I cannot reach the mysterious can. I turn my nose to Fetch Man. He smells like paint and grease and oil. And also like strange humans and coffee and sweat. This can only mean one thing—he's been at the tool store! This cannot be good.

Food Lady peers inside the bag and pulls out little squares of shaggy rug. Rectangles of fabric. Brushes of different sizes. And stiff paper that's gritty and sort of sparkly. She gazes at Fetch Man, her brow furrowed, like maybe she was expecting a treat instead of all this useless stuff. "Really?" she asks.

Fetch Man rubs his hands together, full of

excitement. He grabs the long pole and spongy roller as if he can't wait to play with them.

While he and Food Lady chatter with each other, I glance over at Hattie. She's sipping her milk like she wants it to last forever. "Nana coming," Fetch Man says.

"Yes-but," Food Lady says.

Every time Fetch Man says "Nana," Hattie's gaze drops to the floor. I hear her mutter "Hattie-the-Grrate" under her breath. She's definitely worried. Or nervous. But why? We love Nana!

Food Lady sighs. She hands the big, heavy can back to Fetch Man, who heads into the hall. I'm tempted to follow, but then Food Lady opens a cabinet and pulls out a loaf of bread.

Whoopee! Lunch! My tail twirls in anticipation. I rush to Food Lady's side, hoping for delicious crumbs to fall.

Food Lady cocks her head when she sees how sad Hattie looks. She goes over and pats her shoulder.

Hattie doesn't look up. "Hattie-the-Grrate," she mumbles again.

"Oh, bay-bee," Food Lady says. She speaks to Hattie in a voice that's encouraging and hopeful. But also like she's giving Hattie a job to do. "You-can-do-it."

She must be urging Hattie to finish that milk, because

that's what she does. Hattie's still not smiling, but she kisses Food Lady's cheek, clanks her glass in the sink, and trudges out of the room.

I start to go after her, but right then Food Lady goes to the tall, frosty box. Where the peanut butter lives. And jelly!

But Hattie's already down the hall and turning toward the stairs. I have to find out what she's doing.

Ignoring my drooling tongue, I hightail it through the hallway and chase Hattie upstairs. At the top, I see something that makes me pause—the empty room.

The place with horrible memories. Where I get trapped behind The Gate all alone when my humans are mad. The empty room is the worst place in the whole house!

Except it's not empty anymore.

Old sheets are scattered on the floor, that big can sitting in the middle. Fetch Man's on a stepladder beside the window, sticking tape around the edges. It's the very definition of mysterious.

I charge in to investigate!

"FEN-way, stop!" Fetch Man snaps, mopping his sweaty face with his T-shirt.

I skid to a halt, a sheet bunching under my paws. I was only doing my job. This place needs to be checked out. What if that ladder is dangerous? What if that big can is full of something yucky, like beans?

Fetch Man glares at me. He points at the doorway. "Out!" he says, his face serious and urgent.

Whoa, easy, Fetch Man. It's not like somebody chewed your new shoes. Or ate a whole meat loaf! I back into the hall before he goes completely bonkers.

Even though it looks different and it's not empty anymore, that room is clearly still full of yelling and punishments. Good thing I found out before I accidentally got trapped in there again.

I follow Hattie's scent to her room. Sure enough, she's sitting on the floor, gazing at the Nana-box, her face scrunched.

I assume growl position. While keeping my distance. "Get back in the closet, you terrible box!" I snarl, baring my teeth. "Nobody wants you here!"

Hattie rubs a hand over it. She looks cautious and confused, like she can't decide if she loves it or hates it. And she smells nervous. Obviously, she needs my help.

I jump up and slobber her cheek. "Trust me on this, Hattie," I bark. "This thing is bad news. Let's go bury it in the closet again."

"Aw, Fenway," she says with a weak smile.

I lick her cheek again. "It'll take two seconds. When it comes to burying things, I'm a professional."

She pets my head for a while, like she's considering it.

"That's my girl." I snuggle her shoulder. "Our favorite games are way better than that new one."

I'm probably getting through to her, but she still smells worried. She heaves a heavy sigh. What is her strange fascination with the Nana-box? Why can't she just leave it alone?

Right then, Fetch Man pops his head in the doorway, and we both turn. "Lunch," he says.

Wowee! I knew it was lunchtime! I spring up and spin in circles.

I follow Hattie into the hall. When she ducks into the Bathtub Room, I hang back on the safety of the carpet. I shudder, thinking of what the ladies said. Hattie can splash herself with that rushing water and smelly soap all she wants, as long as it doesn't involve me.

After she reappears, we're heading toward the stairs when I come face-to-face with . . .

THE GATE!

When did that go up?

All of a sudden, it's guarding the doorway to the empty room. Hattie leans over, her head poking into

26

the room. My ears droop with punishment memories. "Don't even think about it, Hattie!" I bark, nudging her toward the stairs. "There's nothing good in there."

She scoops me up and nuzzles her face in my fur. I've won another round. But with the way scary things keep popping up around here, I'm going to have to stay on my game.

@Hapter 5

In the Eating Place, Fetch Man and Food Lady gobble their sandwiches in record time. But Hattie's apparently got higher priorities. After only one or two bites, she sneaks the rest of hers under the table into my waiting jaws.

Chomp! Mmmmm! Peanut butter and jelly is my favorite. I rub against her shin. "Best buddies, best buddies," I croon.

Hattie smiles and pats my head, but she still doesn't smell happy. "Best buddies, best buddies," she sings.

When the Eating Place is clean and every crumb's been licked off the floor, we head back upstairs. The empty room is still guarded by The Gate, but it's not empty for long. Fetch Man and Food Lady emerge from their room wearing their oldest, rattiest clothes. Giving us stern words of warning, they climb over The Gate and disappear.

I want to hang around and see what they're doing, but Hattie has other plans. She snatches me up and carries me into her room.

With a loud breath, she plops onto her cozy bed. She scratches behind my ears—Ah, yeah! That's the spot—but judging by the blank look in her eyes, she's busy thinking.

We're quiet for a minute or two, until a loud, happy voice drifts through the window screen. Hattie props her elbows on the ledge. I climb onto her lap and peer outside.

Our Dog Park looks empty and boring, but the one next door is the exact opposite. The ladies are chasing a ball that Angel is tossing. "Go get it!" she calls.

Hattie perks up, smelling excited. She's getting an idea.

My tail swishes. Wowee! I bet I've got the exact same idea!

"Angel!" Hattie calls out the window. She chatters a bit, then rushes over to the Nana-box. "Fenway, come!" she grunts.

My tail wilts, and I back away. "My idea was to go outside and play with our friends. Not with this thing!"

Hattie wheels the scary Nana-box into the hall. Where is she going? Is she planning to toss that thing into the trash?

I have to find out. I'm bounding after her when I start to gag. Eeeee-yew! The hallway's suddenly filled with the overpowering odor of paint. I have to get out of here!

Hattie calls to the tall humans in a hurried voice as we pass by. The box must be heavy, because it thumps down the stairs. And Hattie's breathing is more strained than usual. Downstairs, I trail her through the hallway to the back door.

As Hattie slides it open, my tail starts swishing again. Hooray! Hooray! At least we had the same idea about going outside! Maybe I can convince Hattie to ditch the box and play fetch with our friends.

She lugs the box onto the porch, and I zip into the grass, leaping and twirling with anticipation. Because I hear our friends coming!

Hattie looks over at the Friend Gate as it swings open. "Angel!" she calls.

The ladies rush into our Dog Park, Angel trotting in behind them. She's still clutching that ball, but she's got something else, too—a small bag. The kind that snacks come in. Yippee! I'm always ready for snacks!

I leap up and give it a few sniffs. *Mmmmm!* It smells like peanut butter. I love peanut butter!

The ladies come up for the circle-sniff dance. "'Sup, ladies?" I say.

Goldie turns her head toward Hattie and Angel, who are hovering over the Nana-box on the porch. "What's that?" she asks as we all head over.

I'm way more interested in Angel's bag. I leap at her hand. Wowee! It smells really peanut-y. "Just a box full of silky scarves and random stuff that isn't much fun," I say.

Goldie cocks her head, studying the box. "Not much fun?" she says. "Are you sure about that?"

Hattie goes to shoo me down, but Angel giggles and opens the bag. "Ready, Fenway?" she says.

"I'm so ready! I'm so ready!" I bark, jumping and begging.

Angels pulls something out of the bag. Probably a treat! She peels off a crackle-y shell. I can hardly wait to eat it!

I leap wildly. Hooray! Hooray! Something yummy is coming!

Angel tosses the treat into my mouth . . .

Chomp—ew! It feels like a pebble. I roll it around on my tongue. *Patooey!* I spit it onto the porch.

Goldie nods at it with a look of recognition. "I could've warned you it was a peanut."

I gaze at the slobbery pebble. It smells like peanut butter, but it's definitely something foul. "A peanut?"

Hattie and Angel exchange shrugs. They each crack open a peanut and pop them into their mouths, bits of shell falling onto the floor.

Well, that wasn't nearly as great as I thought it was going to be. Obviously, we need to find something better to do. I romp down the steps in search of a keep-away twig.

But when I find one, Goldie and Patches are still on the porch. They gaze at the short humans with rapt attention.

Hattie adjusts the tall hat on her head. She ties the cape around her shoulders. "Sho-Nana," she says. "Hattie-the-Grrate." Angel smiles and looks on with approval.

Hattie flips through the pages of a little book, Angel hunching over her shoulder. They ooh and aah like that book is the most interesting thing they've ever seen.

Angel takes the tall hat and punches her fist through the top. Whoa! She broke Hattie's hat.

But Hattie doesn't seem the slightest bit angry. Actually, she grins and nods at Angel like this is exactly what she was expecting. She grabs the fake flowers and stuffs them into the hat, clearly eager to play with them. Hattie taps the hat with the stick. "Ab-ra-ca-dab-ra!" She pulls the flowers back out, saying, "Ta-da!"

Angel laughs and claps. Hattie takes a bow. For the first time since the humans started saying "Nana" all the time, Hattie looks hopeful.

What changed her mind about this stuff? Maybe this Nana-box is only fun for two short humans playing together? Or one short human and one Nana? It's certainly no fun for dogs!

Because everybody knows what's fun for dogs is romping around the Dog Park playing fetch or keep-away. So why are the ladies standing on the porch watching Hattie and Angel? I slink over, dropping the twig on the porch.

Right then, Patches turns to Goldie. "I know what this is!" she says. "Remember when those short humans came over with pretty packages?"

Goldie grimaces. "You mean when they ran around screaming? And tossing balloons that exploded with water?"

"No. Well, yes," Patches says. "I was thinking about the stranger who showed up in the tall hat and the black cape."

Goldie squints at the short humans. "The box he

brought was much larger than that one," she says. "But I do remember a similar black stick. And that funny word 'ab-ra-ca-dab-ra.'"

"And a white bird that popped out of his hat," Patches says.

"As I recall, it was a bunny," Goldie corrects. "And the short humans whooped and cheered."

I shudder. A bunny's the last thing I'd want to see pop out of anybody's hat.

"The point is they thought the animal appeared out of nowhere," Patches says. "When the scent was obviously under the table the whole time."

"I knew the guy was putting on an act from the first moment I smelled him," Goldie huffs.

Patches gives her a nudge. "Was that before or after he bribed you with that cookie?"

"What?" Goldie sounds shocked. "I'm pretty sure you were the one greedily wolfing down treat after treat."

"Who am I to refuse kindness from a stranger?" Patches says.

"Well, what about when he stowed Angel in that fake cabinet?" Goldie says. "They all thought she was missing when she was there the whole time."

He put Angel in a cabinet? *Gulp.* That's too much like Hattie stuffing me in the Nana-box and shutting the lid tight.

Patches shakes her head. "When Angel popped out, everyone gasped with delight."

"Short humans are easily fooled," Goldie says. "Dogs are too clever to fall for such silly tricks."

Silly tricks? Is that all it is? I peer over at Hattie tapping the tall hat with the black stick. "Abracadabra!" she shouts again. She reaches into the hat and pulls out the fake flowers.

Angel laughs and claps just as hard as last time.

I heave a sigh of relief. Hattie's happy again. The ladies are right—short humans are easily amused. Dogs are too smart to be fooled by tricks, and besides, there's no way I'm going back in that box. Clearly, there's nothing to be worried about.

I look at Goldie and Patches and drop down on my forepaws. "Now, how about a game of keep-away?" I chomp the twig and tear down the steps into the grass.

They can't resist! Tails flapping, the ladies take off in hot pursuit. The game is on!

I run from one end of the Dog Park to the other, my fur rippling in the breeze. Goldie and Patches are going to need some serious legs to keep up with me! I'm whizzing along the bushes—which sound buzzy for some reason—when a blur zooms past. It's kind of stripe-y, and its cheeks are fat and bulging. It's that chipmunk! What's he got in those cheeks, stolen goods?

I drop the stick. "Time out, ladies!" I call, pivoting. I tear after that chipmunk as he plunges under a bush. "Stop, thief!"

There's no response. And no sign of him besides the stench. I paw the dirt and—

Bzzzzz! Bzzzzz! Bzzzzz!

Hey, what the—?!

CHAPTER 6

YOWZA!

I back out from the bush, my white paw buckling under me. Bits of leaves and twigs cling to my fur. "Fire! Fire!" I howl. "My paw is on fire!"

Goldie and Patches race over, panting. "I don't see any smoke," Goldie says. "Or flames."

Patches cocks her head and listens. "But there is definitely a lot of buzzing going on."

Goldie focuses on the bushes. "Probably bees," she says, backpedaling.

Bees?! Who said anything about bees? My paw is on fire! I leap—no, hop—frantically through the grass, my white paw refusing to move. And it's throbbing. I give it a couple of licks. And then a couple hundred more.

Patches trots up to me. "What's with the paw, Fenway?" she asks.

"I told you, it's ON FIRE!" I scream. "My paw's being burned to a crisp!"

"Fenway," she says gently. "I think you've been stung."

Stung? I don't think so. I jump around on three legs. "It's on fire, I tell you! Fire! Fire!"

Goldie and Patches huddle together, talking. But they don't do anything about the fire. What's wrong with them? We're all in terrible danger!

I'm vaguely aware of Hattie and Angel calling from the porch. But I can't stop to listen. All that matters is my white paw. It's pulsing and burning. And what's this? It's puffing up! I drop down and lick, lick, lick . . .

I give it everything I've got! That burn is fierce, but I'm fiercer!

"Fenway!" Hattie is at my side. How long has she been here? Her voice is concerned, her arms are reaching.

I hop away from her. "No thanks, Hattie! I'm way too busy to snuggle!" I howl. "The bottom of my paw is on fire and I need to lick it!"

Hattie is undeterred. "Fenway!" she calls, more

forcefully this time. She must really want to snuggle. I try to dodge out of the way, but her hands are too swift. They grasp my torso and lift me up.

I start to protest but quickly stop with an amazing realization. In Hattie's arms, my tongue can reach my paw pads more easily! *Slurp, slurp, slurp* . . . I must lick that terrible hurt!

Suddenly, Angel is here, too. And we're all rushing to the house.

Craning my neck, I spot Goldie and Patches curled up near the giant tree in the back of the Dog Park. They look like they're trying to disappear.

Hattie cradles me in her arms. "Aw, Fenn-waay," she says. Her voice is full of sympathy. She smells sad and hurt.

Welcome to the pack, Hattie! I'm pretty sad and hurt, too! *Ow-oh-ooooow! Slurp . . . slurp . . . slurp . . .*

"Hattie?" Food Lady's voice calls from the upper window.

Hattie hoists me up. "Help!" she yells at Food Lady. "Uh-BEE!"

Food Lady's loud "Oh no!" drifts into the Dog Park as Hattie hurries up the porch steps. Next thing I know, we are tearing through the house.

Fetch Man and Food Lady appear in the hallway,

reeking of paint. Fetch Man reaches for my white paw.

Ow! I yank out of his grasp, curling my paw against my throat. "Keep your hands to yourself!" I yelp.

Hattie turns, shielding me from Fetch Man's grabby hands. Thank you, Hattie! You're the one I can count on. *Slurp, slurp, slurp . . .*

I'm so focused on licking my paw, I barely see Fetch Man talking into his hand. "Now!" he snaps.

Keys jingle. We're in the garage. Fetch Man opens the car door. Me and Hattie bound into the back seat.

Normally, riding in the car is very exciting—sticking my head out the window, the rush of air hitting my face, my nostrils pulsing with thrilling scents. Normally, I'd go nuts wondering where we're going. Maybe someplace interesting. Or delicious.

But none of those things is happening. This is no normal ride in the car. All I want to do is curl up in Hattie's lap and lick, lick, lick that awful fire away. *Slurp, slurp, slurp . . .*

We zoom. We cruise. We turn. We stop.

Hattie flings the door open, and we race up to a building that looks like a store.

But it doesn't have big windows like a store. And it doesn't smell like a store, either.

It smells like dogs . . . and cats . . . and . . . FEAR.

My fur tingles. This place reminds me of somewhere I've been before. Someplace scary. I think about making a run for it. But it's too late. We're already inside.

A dog growls. "Let me at him!"

A caged cat hisses.

We go up to a counter with treats on it. Treats?

A lady human greets us like she knew we'd show up. We trail her into a tiny room. And chills tingle up my spine.

The room reeks of terror and agony and doom. On one wall is a picture of dogs with lots of bones—*inside* their bodies. And worse—another wall has a metal table with no legs.

I know this table. It goes up and down. Claws scrape and slide on it. Like the Table of Panic at the vet's office in our old neighborhood.

Uh-oh. There couldn't be more than one vet's office, could there?

Now I really want to bolt!

But before I can make a move, the side door opens and in walks another lady. She's wearing a white coat. Dark hair is piled loosely on top of her head. Her eyes are wide and kind. She smells friendly. She speaks to us with breath that smells spicy, like cinnamon. She's gazing at me intently . . . in a way that's disturbing.

Extremely disturbing.

Because she's looking at my white paw. Just like Hattie and Fetch Man did at home. If Spicy Breath thinks she's touching this paw, she's going to be very disappointed.

I press against Hattie's chest. "Keep this lady away from me! She's got evil on her mind!"

Spicy Breath comes at me.

But Hattie doesn't move. "Shhh," she whispers, kissing my head.

"Can't you see she's headed this way?" I bark, my hind legs kicking. "Let's get out of here! Before it's too late!"

Hattie still doesn't move. She gazes at me, her eyes glassy and wet. She smells upset.

And then to my gut-wrenching horror, she hands me over.

CHAPTER 7

I turn to my short human, my eyes pleading.
"Help me!"

But Hattie just looks away.

Spicy Breath grabs me tight. She wraps me in a hug, like we're friends!

Hello! She's clearly anything but! Besides cinnamon, she smells like fear—from other dogs, cats, and even bunnies. A terrifying combination!

I thrash. I squirm. I must get free! "Release me! This is a big mistake!" I yowl. "I just want to lick my paw in peace!"

Fetch Man calmly looks on. Hattie leans against him, her face sad and hopeful. Do they seriously not realize their dog is in trouble?

Spicy Breath's grip is so strong, there's no way to escape. All my kicking manages to do is bunch up her coat.

I growl and snap. "Put me down, lady! I mean business!"

Next thing I know, I'm on the Table of Panic. The one that goes up and down! Spicy Breath leans in. Her grip tightens. Clearly, she's got evil on her mind!

"Fenn-waay! Fenn-waay!"

I whip around. Hattie's grinning at me. At last, she's come to her senses!

But her smile is way too huge. And she smells anxious. Very anxious. Talk about bad signs.

Hattie's fingers reach out. *Sniff . . . sniff . . .* Hmm, she has a treat. And she's waving it right in front of my nose.

Chomp! Mmmmm. That was so yum—Hey!

Click. What's this?! My jaws are clamped shut! My mouth won't open. I've been muzzled!

I swipe at the straps, but it's no use. This thing won't come off! How will I bark? How will I eat? And worst of all, how will I lick my burning paw?!

I'm the very definition of panicked! I shake and shudder. I kick and thrash. I have to do something! I will not give up!

Hattie hovers. "Best buddies, best buddies," she sings,

even though we're not cuddling and it's not bedtime. Her voice catches, and she doesn't smell the least bit happy. She must feel bad. She must want to help!

Is there still hope? I nuzzle her arm. I gaze up at her with pathetic eyes. But all she does is kiss the top of my head again. Like that could possibly change anything.

All I can do is whimper. And shake.

Because Fetch Man grips my lower body. Spicy Breath's got me in a headlock. I feel a pinch behind my neck . . .

Hattie scratches behind my ears. "Aw, Fenway," she coos. There's something awfully suspicious about her tone. And she's acting funny, too. She keeps glancing up at Spicy Breath. Like a dog waiting for a command.

Could that actually be what's happening? Hattie taking commands from Spicy Breath?

It's too terrible to consider. Besides, I have to concentrate. I have to keep fighting. Which I must be doing pretty hard, because—*whew*. Am I ever tired . . .

I feel myself relaxing, dropping down on the table. My eyelids droop. And then . . .

I suck in a long, deep breath. I'm no longer on the Table of Panic. I'm lounging outside in the Dog Park, luxuriating in the lush, cool grass. Aaaaah!

Lovely sunshine bathes my coat. A soft breeze tickles my nostrils. A bright light flashes in my eyes.

47

Oh no! A flashing light means thundering BOOM-KABOOMS are coming!

I brace myself for the horrible noises. I shiver with bravery. I must find the used-to-be bear. And a place to hide!

But before I can make a move, I hear something that's not loud at all.

A sound that's quiet. And soothing. It sounds like Hattie's sweet voice.

"Fenway!" she cries happily. She's running through the grass, waving at me.

Yippee! I bound toward her, my tail swishing with glee.

Hattie crouches down. "Fenn-waay," she calls, her outstretched arms inviting me to bound right in.

I can't wait to feel her embrace. To lose myself in her soothing voice. To bask in the glow of her loving devotion.

She rushes closer. I catch a whiff of her special scent—mint and vanilla. And something else, too. Not wonderful dirt . . . something yucky. And spicy.

Cinnamon?

Why does Hattie smell different? Well, there's no time to think. She's almost here. I'm ready to leap into her arms!

She's so close. I want to bark for joy! I go to open my jaws . . . but they're clamped shut. They won't open! Where did this muzzle come from?

And worse than that—where is Hattie?

I stop in my tracks. She was just here. She couldn't have vanished. Her smell is everywhere.

My head swivels, searching . . .

"Fenn-waay!" Hattie sings.

I spin around. And around. And then—I spot her! Her head is poking out from the bushes!

Hooray! She'll get rid of this muzzle and then I can slobber her cheeks with love and appreciation! But first, I need to get over to those bushes.

I bolt across the Dog Park, straight toward her beaming face. She's obviously very excited. And why not? She wants to adore her loyal dog. And she's about to get her wish!

But as I cruise up to the bushes—poof! Hattie's head disappears. I plunge under the low branches. I have to find her!

I tremble with panic. My heart aches for Hattie. I need her! I have to find her!

I'm running frantically around the Dog Park. I'm fearing the worst. But then I hear the door sliding open. It's Hattie! She's striding onto the porch!

But as I spring up the steps, my heart drops to my paws. Hattie's wearing a white coat. Her hair is piled loosely on top of her head. Her eyes are wide and kind. And she smells like dogs and cats and . . . fear. And where did all that cinnamon come from?

I shudder. Because Hattie looks exactly like a certain Spicy Breath lady that I'd rather not think about. And also she's staring at my white paw. With an expression of pure evil.

I curl my paw in protectively. I limp away as fast as I can on three legs.

But when I reach the bottom step—yikes! I'm face-to-face with Spicy Breath! I swivel back to the porch. Oh no! She's there, too!

There are two of her? No—three! Another Spicy Breath pops up behind me! I'm surrounded. And outnumbered!

The Spicy Breaths have got me covered. I want to cry out. I want to protect myself. But my jaws are strapped shut.

All I can do is huddle. Make myself into a tight ball. And whine.

Hands close around my neck. Snap!

And when I look up, my head is encased in plastic.

Chapter 8

When my eyes flutter open, I'm looking at smooth plastic. Everywhere.

And something's stuck around my neck. A new collar? A really tall collar? It's taller than my whole head.

I swipe at it. I shake my head. I swipe some more, but this thing won't budge. What's going on?

Where am I? I can't see from side to side. I start to pant. My own steamy breath hits me in the face. I shake some more, and plastic bangs the sides of my head. This can only be one thing—a Cone of Doom!

I'd heard stories back at the Dog Park. I almost remember when I was a tiny puppy . . . but I never—

"Fenway . . ." Hattie's soothing voice. Her loving hand on my back.

Whew! Suddenly, everything is clear. We're not outside in the Dog Park. And no Spicy Breaths are here. According to my nose, we're in the back of the car and Fetch Man's in front. And according to my ears, the car has just gone quiet.

"Hattie, I'm so glad you're here!" I bark. "There's a—a—cone on my head!" It must be some kind of mix-up. I didn't even do anything wrong.

Humming softly, Hattie keeps patting my back. Clearly, she approves of my efforts to ditch the cone. Not that they're doing any good.

I twist my whole body so I can look at her. She's the same old Hattie, smiling at me. I sigh with relief. She's the same as always. And she smells like mint and vanilla, like she's supposed to. Was I expecting something else?

I try to shake a weird feeling. Why is my head trapped in the Cone of Doom?

I rub against Hattie. "How about a little help?"

The car door opens. Hattie springs out, holding me tight. "Shhh, Fenway," she murmurs. I smell our garage. I hear the door unlatch.

Hattie whisks me into the Eating Place, her concerned face peering into the cone. Her eyes are huge and sad. What does she have to feel sad about? I'm the one in the Cone of Doom!

I wipe it on her shoulder. "In case you haven't noticed, this thing won't come off!" I whine.

"Awwwww," she says. Her hand reaches in and pets my snout.

Next thing I know, I'm on her lap again. And we're . . . on a chair? For real?

Wowee! Are my eyes playing tricks on me? Me and Hattie are sitting at the table in the Eating Place. I've always wanted to be up here! *Sniff . . . sniff . . .* My nose goes nuts.

The table's completely empty, except for one tiny crumb of toast. It's way across from us.

I'm about to sneak onto the table and get it when familiar scents swarm around me like flies. Fetch Man's arm swims into view. Food Lady's shirt. Uh-oh.

They've spotted us! Now we're in trouble! I cower against Hattie's chest, bracing myself for the yelling and shooing me off Hattie's seat.

But there are no yells. No shoos. When the tall humans do speak, their voices are kind.

"Fenn-waay," Food Lady says, her worried face peering into the cone.

Fetch Man peeks in, too. "Hey, fella." His smile is a little too forced.

I shrink back. Something is wrong with this picture.

Why are my humans being so nice to me? I'm sitting at the table, an unforgivable offense. Usually, punishments come after the crime. Is the Cone of Doom a punishment in advance?

That doesn't make sense. But what could be its purpose? And why aren't my humans shooing me away from the table?

There's no doubt about it—something very suspicious is going on.

And I'll figure it out right after I lick my white paw, which is suddenly itching like crazy. I try to bring it up to my mouth and—Hey! The cone is in the way. Now I really have to ditch it. Like right now!

I swipe at the cone, but it's still not going anywhere. How hard could it be to slip out of this thing?

I'm about to ask Hattie for help again when Food Lady says, "Treat?"

My tail thumps. "Yes, please!" We'll get the cone off right after I eat.

Hattie carries me over to the counter. Fetch Man opens a little box. It's awfully small for a box of treats. And it doesn't smell like treats. What could it be?

Fetch Man pulls out a tiny bottle and twists off the top, revealing a dropper. I give it a few sniffs.

Ewwwww! I know what this is—yucky drops!

I turn my head in protest. I'm about to tell Fetch Man there's no way I'm going to gulp those things down when I hear a much more promising sound.

Hattie opens another, much bigger box. The right kind of box! The one that rattles. And smells like beefy treats!

My tail comes back to life. A treat really is coming. Hooray!

Hattie grabs a crunchy-looking, delicious-smelling treat. My tongue drips. My tummy rumbles. "I'm so ready! I'm so ready!" I bark.

Her eyes full of pity, Hattie tosses the treat into my mouth.

Chomp! Mmmmm! Wowee, it sure is tasty. "More, please," I bark.

Right on cue, Hattie grabs another treat. My tail goes berserk. But instead of tossing the treat into my watering mouth, Hattie offers it to Fetch Man. Huh? Is he going to eat it?

"Here, Fenway," Hattie says in a sweet voice. She turns me around.

Hey, I can't see Fetch Man. What if he wolfs down my treat?

Hattie thrusts her fingers inside the cone and waves the treat in front of my nose.

Ew! It smells yucky! My jaws clamp shut. What happened to that perfectly good treat?

"Fenn-waay . . . Fenn-waay . . ." Hattie says, even more sweetly this time. "Yum-yum!" She waggles the treat against my mouth. Which is closed tight.

I turn away. What can Hattie be thinking? Why is she trying to coax me into eating that yucky treat?

"Mmmmm-mmmmm, Fenway," Fetch Man hums, much too eagerly.

"Come on, Fenway," Food Lady chimes in.

I twist in protest. Why is everybody ganging up on me? Do they really think I'm that gullible? Don't they know I can smell how yucky it is?

Fetch Man taps his foot. Food Lady sighs.

Hattie speaks to them in a frustrated tone. She sets the yucky treat on the counter.

At last, she's given up! I swivel back around. Or has she? Fetch Man hands her the tiny bottle. He gives her an encouraging look. "Go on," he says.

Hattie smells determined and anxious at the same time. She takes out the dropper and points it at my mouth.

"Oh no you don't!" I bark, squirming and curling away. "Those drops are not coming anywhere near me!"

"FEN-way!" Hattie scolds, gripping me tight.

Fetch Man grabs me by the neck. He forces my cone-head around, toward that pointy dropper!

I thrash wildly. "No! No! You can't make me!"

My jaws clench, but it's too late. Hattie somehow shoved the yucky dropper in. Before I realize what's happening, slimy liquid oozes into my mouth.

Eeeee-yooooow! Is that ever yucky, yucky, yucky!

"Okay, fella," Fetch Man says, patting me on the back like everything's fine. I hear him and Food Lady shuffle out of the Eating Place and pad upstairs.

Hattie's putting the dropper back in the bottle when *tap! tap! tap!* comes from the back door. "Hattie?" Angel's voice calls through the screen.

Hattie sets me down and rushes over to her.

Paaaaatooey! I gag those drops right out of my mouth.

CHapteR 9

Once every bit of those yucky drops is
on the floor, I hobble after Hattie and out the door. I
turn the Cone of Doom toward the sky and quickly turn
away, squinting. How did the light get so blinding? And
why is the breeze ruffling my coat but not my ears?

Chipper, chatter, squawk!

My hackles shoot up. Those sounds can only mean
one thing—a squirrel! I turn my head one way, then the
other, but there's no sign of him. All I can see is what's
right in front of me.

I swivel my cone-head to check out the porch, one
tiny section at a time. The Nana-box is wide open. Balls,
rings, and fake flowers are strewn all over the table.
More stuff is piled on the floor.

"Ta-da!" I zero in on Hattie's voice. She picks up the tall hat and plops it on her head, squishing down her bushy hair. She bows, the cape whipping over her shoulder as Angel claps and cheers.

Hattie smiles like everything is right and nothing is wrong. I shudder. What was the deal with the yucky drops? Why is she acting like that never happened? And has she not noticed that there's a cone on my head that needs to come off?

"Fenway?" Angel says. My cone-head snaps in her direction. She's speaking to Hattie, but she's looking at me. And saying my name.

My hopes soar. Are they going to play with me? Or better yet, are they about to rescue me from this Cone of Doom so I can lick my itchy paw?

Yippee! I hobble toward them on three legs—*oof!* I bump into something . . . a chair? Where did that come from?

As soon as I turn around, Hattie is already distracted by the Nana-toys. She picks up the abracadabra stick and flips through the little book with great interest. While her dog is right here, needing help! Has she forgotten about me?

I'm about to remind her of the problem when I hear Patches's lovely voice. "Fenway?"

In the Dog Park next door, tags jingle. Paws lope

through the Friend Gate. Hooray! Hooray! The ladies are coming!

I rush down the porch steps, and—*whoa-oh-oooooh! Splat!* I belly flop onto the grass.

I hop up and give myself a good shake. The cone shifts, smacking me in the face. *Ow!* Bad news—it's still on tight.

I hear Goldie pad over. "Wow, that's quite the cone you've got there."

"Oh my goodness, Fenway," Patches says after they've both given me a round of sniffs. "Look at you."

I give my head another shake. "This Cone of Doom won't come off!"

Patches cocks her head and studies me for a moment. "Well, I'm pretty sure it's not supposed to."

I drop down and bring my itchy white paw for a good licking, and—*oof!*—it bangs into the cone. Again!

Goldie noses in. "So what happened?"

"That's a great question." I gape at the ladies, trying to remember. "There was a ride in the car . . . and a place . . . with panicking animals." I shiver at the scary memory. "The wall had a picture of dogs with bones—*inside* their bodies! It—it—it reeked of fear and torture!"

Goldie and Patches exchange a look of disbelief.

"Believe me, it was the Worst Place Ever." My mind

is swirling with horrible images, each one more terrible than the last. "There was a Spicy Breath in a white coat—no, wait! There were two or maybe even three of her. And they all had gigantic fangs and claws and sharp, sharp needles!"

Goldie scrunches her face. "Spicy breaths? In white coats?"

Patches gawks. "Gigantic fangs? And claws?"

"I'm telling you, it was worse than a nightmare!"

Goldie looks at me sideways. "Or maybe it actually *was* a nightmare?"

"Look at me! This Cone of Doom is proof." I thrust out my chest. "My paw was on fire even though I licked and licked. And before I could make it better, Spicy Breath came at me with her wicked fangs and claws. It was horrifying!"

Patches gazes at me with kind eyes. "Sounds like you were awfully upset."

"Wouldn't you be?" I gulp as it all—or at least some of it—comes back to me. "I wanted to run away, but there was no escape. They grabbed me, held me down, and then . . . Well, I can't remember everything. But it was all very, very bad. And my head ended up trapped in this cone!"

Goldie glances up at the porch, then back at me.

"And where were your humans during this horrendous experience?"

I blink a few times. "Why, Hattie was with me, of course."

"And she tried to help you escape, right?" Goldie asks. "Don't tell us she just stood by and watched."

"Naturally she tried to help! Why would you even ask?" I practically shout. "And she'd take this cone off me right now, if she could."

"You think so?" Goldie asks, her voice more than a little bit skeptical.

Patches gives her a look of disapproval, then turns to me. "Maybe you shouldn't focus so much on getting it off, Fenway. It's not really so bad, is it?"

I glare at her. "Easy for you to say, Patches. I don't see a cone on your head!"

"Oh, but I do know," she says gently. "We've all been there—waking up with a cone, furless spot on the belly, humans fussing and saying a strange word. 'Spade,' I believe it was. But in any case, the time passes quickly. And then, before you know it, the cone is gone and everything is back to normal."

"Speak for yourself," Goldie says. "You slept the whole time. Me, I stared out the window, wondering why we weren't going out to play."

Patches frowns. "Yes, but you told me you enjoyed all that extra love and attention. You said our precious Angel couldn't do enough for you, remember?"

Goldie cocks her head. "I said that?"

"This is totally different!" I yell. "My belly isn't furless. My paw needs to be licked! And—Wait, did you say something about extra love and attention?"

"Why, yes," Patches says. "It's a well-known fact that short humans hate to see a dog suffer. But the point is—"

"So you're saying I can use this to my advantage?" A brilliant idea forms in my mind.

Goldie starts grumbling. Patches begins a speech. Something about patience. But I turn away. I'm too busy thinking . . .

A few moments later, I'm about to thank the ladies for their help and rush over to Hattie when I hear a horrible sound. Coming from the porch.

Chip-chip-chip!

My ears tingle. I know that sound—that thieving chipmunk! I limp toward the porch, my whole body on high alert.

As I approach, he shoots out from under the porch. His tail straight up, menacingly. His cheeks fat and bulging—obviously filled with loot!

"Halt, you crook!" I bark. "Or pay the consequences!"

He races through the grass, ignoring my vicious warning. He's heading for the bushes. What a lame strategy! We've played this game before.

Maybe I can't run, but I can head him off. I get to the bushes first, baring my teeth. "Let's see you get past me, coward!"

Apparently, that's what he's about to do. He heads straight at me, darting to one side, then zipping to the other. And suddenly—Hey! Where'd he go?

I swivel my head, but he's vanished. I hear him . . . I smell him . . . which can only mean one thing—he's under the bushes.

I go to dive in after him, but—*oof!* The Cone of Doom won't fit through the branches. Talk about an obstacle!

"Poor guy," I hear Patches mutter.

"He'll have to learn the hard way," Goldie says.

I tune them out. They are not helping. Besides, chipmunk sounds are assaulting my ears. From the other end of the bushes.

Chip-chip-chip!

Does that thieving chipmunk think he can outsmart a professional guard dog like me? I hobble over—Whoa! My paws buckle under and—*splat!* I'm crumpled in the grass.

But not for long. I spring up and limp to the other end of the bushes. I have a job to do!

I stop and listen. This end of the bushes sounds different.

Bzzzzz! Bzzzzz!

Uh-oh. Something tells me I'm better off going the other way.

I start to hobble back to where I was before and—*ow!* I stumble over a stick—then I hear a very different sound.

I turn in the direction of Hattie's triumphant voice. "Abracadabra!" she shouts, her voice full of importance. She reaches into her cape and pulls out a bunch of fake flowers. "Ta-da!"

Angel hoots and claps, looking impressed.

Why? She's seen those same flowers loads of times. Is she really thrilled to see Hattie pull them from her cape? Did she think they were gone?

Or could this be some kind of trick?

CHAPTER 10

At supper time, I remember what the ladies said. This Cone of Doom could actually be good for something—extra love and attention.

And it won't be hard to show Hattie how badly I'm suffering. Right now, "suffering" is my middle name!

The marvelous fragrance of sloppy joes has taken over the Eating Place. My family gathers around the table just like always. I'm perched in my usual spot near Hattie. I smack my chops. Those sloppy joes smell sweet and zesty and oh-so-meaty!

I eagerly watch Hattie's every move, whining in despair. Sure enough, her fingers appear by her leg and a delicious-smelling crumble of meat falls to the floor. Wowee, I love delicious-smelling crumbles of meat!

I'm ready to devour it. But where did it go? Did it somehow vanish?

I sweep my cone-head over the area around Hattie's sneakers and—*ouch!* The cone bangs against the chair leg, and I readjust.

Sniff . . . sniff . . . That irresistible scent is so close by. I creep under the table, panting and drooling. Aha! It's right there, next to the table leg, sitting in a lovely splotch of sloppy joe sauce. And it smells sooooo good!

My tongue dripping with anticipation, I lunge and—*crash!* The Cone of Doom bangs on the floor, my mouth inches from the wonderful crumble of meat.

I back up and try again, my jaws snapping, but—*crash!* The cone bumps against the floor again.

I try over and over, but each time it's the same. My tongue isn't long enough to slurp that delightful bit of sloppy joe.

"Unfair! Unfair!" I whine, backing out from under the table. The pain and injustice make my problems all the worse. "I can't chomp that tasty-smelling meat! I can't lick my itchy sore paw! And this Cone of Doom is stuck on my head!"

Hattie leans down and gives me a pat. "Aw, Fenway," she says, her voice filled with pity.

I gaze up, my eyes drooping with misery. "I'm suffering," I wail. "Can't you see how badly I'm suffering?"

Hattie gazes back at me. Her face is full of agony. "I'm hurting! I'm in pain!" I whine. "I'm completely miserable!"

"Aw . . ." Hattie croons. Her eyes are glistening with tears. Clearly, she feels just as bad about the situation as I do. So why isn't she doing anything about it?

My humans keep on eating those delicious-smelling sloppy joes like nothing is wrong. I keep on writhing and moaning at Hattie's feet. My paw is sore and itchy. My tummy is rumbling. I wallow in the horrible mixture of helplessness and hunger. It's the Worst Supper Time Ever.

Eventually, Hattie sets down her fork. She shifts in her seat. So does Food Lady. Whoopee! My supper is coming!

Is my hard work starting to pay off? I spring up, my tail wagging hopefully. I limp behind Food Lady's feet to the counter. Hooray! Hooray! I hear the wondrous sounds of kibble rattling into my dish. My tongue drips in happy anticipation. "I'm so ready! I'm so ready!" I bark.

But when Food Lady sets the dish in front of me, there's a Very Big Problem. I go to dive in and—*ouch!* the cone bangs the floor, and my mouth can't reach the food.

I stretch my snout as far as I can. My tongue thrusts out, ready to lick that tasty supper. But it won't reach.

I stare up at my humans' confused faces. "Bad news!" I whimper. "I'm staaaaarving and I can't eeeeeat!"

Hattie looks at Fetch Man and Food Lady, her eyes full of concern. They all chatter in anxious voices.

Hattie's starting to cave. I know it! Time to get back to work. I cock my cone-head and gaze up at her with my saddest, most pitiful face. "Hattie, I need my supper!" I moan. "You don't want me to go hungry, dooooo you? I'm just a little dog! I need my foooood!"

Hattie turns to Fetch Man and Food Lady again. I must be getting through to her because she's practically moaning with frustration.

I give it all I've got. I hang my cone-head, my whole body sagging in despair. "I can't go on like this," I whimper. "I'm sooooo hungry!"

I hear shuffling noises. Hattie squats beside me, sniffling. Her fingers graze my neck. *R-r-r-r-rip!*

It works! Hattie's got a sheet of plastic in her hands. And my head is cone-free! The rush of possibility is overwhelming!

I give myself a vigorous shake. Yippee! I've been liberated! I knew all that effort would pay off!

I glance at my supper dish, then at my itchy white paw, and then finally at that wonderful crumble of meat near the table leg. I hardly know what to go after first!

Apparently, Hattie wants to decide for me. She slides

my supper dish right up to my snout. "Here, Fenway," she sings, her voice sweet and inviting. "Yum-yum!"

Whoopee! That food looks absolutely scrumptious! My mouth waters with excitement. I'm about to chomp when I stop short. I detect something besides the meaty kibble. Something unexpected. *Sniff . . . sniff . . .* Yucky drops? Sprinkled on my delicious supper?

"Yum-yum," Hattie says again, practically shoving the dish at me.

It doesn't take a Bloodhound to know my food has been tampered with! I gaze up at Hattie's face, and my tummy lurches in dread. Her expression is eager and happy. But her eyes are wary. And she smells nervous. A sure sign of deception!

It's all so horrible. I need to eat my supper without all that yuckiness. I stick my snout into the dish and rummage through the kibble. *Sniff . . . sniff . . . Chomp! Chomp! Chomp!* I manage to gobble a few bites that smell delicious and not yucky.

I root around some more, sniffing and chomping. Soon half the food is gone. What's left in the bowl smells yuck-yuck-yuck!

I glare at the rest. What a waste. It's all so—Hey! I can lick my itchy white paw!

Slurp . . . slurp . . . slurp . . . aaaaah! That's what I'm talking about!

"FEN-way, no!" Hattie shouts, her voice alarmed. Dropping the sheet of plastic, she lunges for me, her hands grabbing.

No way, Hattie! I didn't come this far to let you win. I skitter toward the doorway, Hattie hot on my tail. She's fast, but I have a huge lead. Even on three legs, I easily beat her down the hall.

I want to lie down and lick my paw, but from the look on Hattie's face and the way she's shouting "NO!" it's pretty clear she's determined to stop me. There's only one thing to do—keep on running.

As I scamper into the Lounging Place, Hattie starts gaining on me. I crawl under the low table. All I need is a safe place to hide. Where Hattie can't reach. And I don't have much time.

Because she races right up to me. "Fenway!" she coaxes. "Come!"

My gaze wanders around the Lounging Place, focusing on the puffy chair, the small table—aha! I shimmy out the other side of the low table and dive straight under the couch. Whoa. It sure is dark under here.

But I feel something. Are those Hattie's fingers brushing up against my tail? I creep along the dusty rug through the darkness, around a rumply sock, past a crumpled sheet of paper, a pencil, and a couple of kernels of buttery popcorn. *Chomp! Chomp! Mmmmm!*

I huddle in the way back. Hopefully there's less chance that Hattie can reach me back here and ruin everything.

Which is exactly what she's trying to do. She lifts a corner of the couch skirt, her face peeking through the dim light. "Fenway," she calls, one arm reaching under the couch.

I scrunch up against the wall. When I'm sure she can't get me, I start licking that itchy white paw. *Slurp . . . slurp . . . slurp . . .* aaaaah! Sweet relief!

"Fenway, no!" Hattie yells, her arm extending, stretching . . . But she's still far from reaching me.

Whew. I'm safe!

Slurp . . . slurp . . . slurp . . . Oh, my paw! My itchy white paw! How I've longed to lick, lick, lick you! *Slurp . . . slurp . . . slurp . . .*

"Fenway, no! No! No!" Hattie shouts. It's obvious she wants me to come out so she can put that Cone of Doom back on. Or worse—shove those yucky drops down my throat. And it's equally obvious she's not going to get her wish. She tries to reach me some more, but she quickly gives up. With a very loud groan, she scrambles away and pads out of the room.

Aaaaah! Alone again at last. I keep on licking until my paw is thoroughly soaked. Though still itching! I get back to work, giving it all I've got. *Slurp . . . slurp . . . slurp . . .*

Moments later, I hear Hattie's footsteps approaching. And by the sound of it, she's got Food Lady and Fetch Man with her. Reinforcements!

The couch skirt lifts again, and I look up. In the shadowy light, Hattie's face appears. "Fenn-waay," she coaxes. Her eyes are excited. Her tone is sweet. But she can't fool me. Even from back here I can smell her frustration. And panic.

I go back to licking. *Slurp . . . slurp . . . slurp . . .*

"Fenn-waay," Hattie coos again. But this time, when her hand reaches under the couch, my nose gets a whiff of something yummy.

A treat?

My mouth waters. My tummy rumbles. Wowee, that treat smells tasty. And not yucky at all. I inch toward Hattie's hand for a better sniff.

Sniff . . . sniff . . . It sure smells like a treat all right! I start to go for it but immediately pull back. It's probably a trick! As soon as I munch that treat, she'll snatch me, and that'll be the end of the lick-fest.

Hattie's hand withdraws. I hear a sigh, then Hattie and the tall humans chattering. Which is probably a bad sign. Why don't they go away and leave a poor, itchy dog in peace?

Slurp . . . slurp . . . slurp . . . The couch skirt lifts yet again. Hattie's face reappears, even more determined this time. "Oh, Fenn-waay," she sings. I wait for her hand to reach under the couch with that tantalizing treat, but it's not coming.

Or is it?

My nose detects its yummy scent. It's coming closer. But the hand I see is not Hattie's. It's Fetch Man's.

And it's reaching all the way to my snout. *Sniff . . . sniff . . .* mmmmm! I open my jaws and—*chomp!* Whoopee! Is that ever tasty!

Fingers grip under my collar. I'm skidding across the rug, out from under the couch. Hey! And I'm in the brightness of the Lounging Place. My humans hover over me. Hattie's arms reach around my neck. *Snap!* The Cone of Doom is snug on my head. Licking time is over.

I swivel from Fetch Man to Food Lady to Hattie. All of them are frowning and shaking their heads. Maybe the cone really is some kind of punishment. "What'd I do?" I bark.

The rest of the night is terrible. With the Cone of Doom snug and tight, I can't lick my white paw, which, besides being itchy, is wet and sore, too.

Hattie carries me up to her room despite my very clear protests. The whole upstairs reeks of wet paint. It's overpowering!

With this cone on my head, I can't even bury my snout in the minty, vanilla-smelling blankets. This is all so wrong! Me and Hattie and the used-to-be bear are supposed to be snuggling in bed, and instead my head is resting against cold, hard plastic. I whimper.

I stare up at her pained face. Clearly, she hates seeing me suffer. "Hattie, I'm in agony here!" I whine. "I can't stand it anymooooore!"

"Aw, Fenway," Hattie says. Her voice is gloomy like she's the one with a Very Big Problem. "Best buddies, best buddies," she sings, kissing my brown paw.

I tuck the white one under my chest. I can't even yowl the song.

But I can't give up. She's caving. I know she is. I roll onto my back and cock my head. "Look, Hattie!" I moan. "Your poor dog is sooooo miserable!"

Hattie's eyes are sad and glossy. "Awwwww!" she coos. I've obviously gotten to her.

R-r-r-r-rip!

Whoopee! The Cone of Doom is off! I give my head a couple of shakes. I pounce on Hattie's chest and lick her cheek. "Thank you, Hattie!" I bark. "I knew you'd come through."

As she strokes the top of my head, I go to wrap a paw around the used-to-be bear. But Hattie pulls it away.

"Hey," Hattie murmurs, studying his face. She runs her finger over his remaining button eye, then feels through the blankets as if she's searching for something. "Aha." She holds up a tiny button.

She springs up and sets the used-to-be bear and the button on top of the dresser. Then climbs back into bed.

I want to ask what she did that for, but then I realize I have something more important to do. *Slurp . . . slurp . . . slurp . . .*

@HapteR 11

When the room is filled with morning brightness, my eyelids pop open. My nose breathes in that horrible paint smell. I burrow under Hattie's rumpled blankets, which are awfully damp and slobbery for some reason.

And whoa, is my white paw ever itchy! I get back to licking. *Slurp . . . slurp . . . slurp . . .*

"Fenway?" Hattie mumbles, rubbing her eyes.

Slurp . . . slurp . . . slurp . . .

Hattie scrambles out of bed and grabs a curved sheet of plastic off the floor. She reaches around my neck and—*snap!*

"Hey!" I bark, stumbling through the blankets. What is this Cone of Doom doing back on my head?

Hattie lifts me up and we head downstairs. Ah! It smells good and normal, like eggs and toast.

I beg Hattie to take the cone off, but all she does is make sad faces at me. Why isn't she helping me escape this thing? Do I have to work my tail off every single time?

While my family eats breakfast, I plop near the screen door. "I need to lick my paw, Hattie!" I whine, raising it up for her to see. "It's itching worse than eeeeever!"

Hattie sneaks a few sorry-looking peeks at me, but she doesn't help. She keeps right on eating her toast while Fetch Man and Food Lady chatter away like their pathetic dog isn't even here. Don't they notice how badly I'm suffering?

After the dishes clatter in the sink, Fetch Man and Food Lady hurry upstairs. Hattie rushes over to me as I hear the Friend Gate creak open and bang shut.

I spring up and peer through the door. My tail swings in happy expectation. Our friends are coming! Maybe the ladies can help me out some more.

"Angel!" Hattie cries, and I follow her out onto the porch.

Angel makes a sad face when she sees me and gives me a quick pat. She and Hattie head straight for the Nana-box and start fishing through the toys. I swivel my cone-head, scanning the Dog Park. Where are Goldie and Patches?

After hobbling past the vegetable patch and tending to some daily business, I scout along the side fence. Is it my imagination? Or is that heavy breathing?

I position the Cone of Doom over a gap in the fence. Two black noses appear in my face. Four glossy eyes stare back at me.

"Ladies!" I cry, hopping back in surprise. "What are you doing?"

"What does it look like?" Goldie says. "We're keeping a watch on things."

"Not that we wanted to be nosy, of course," Patches explains before pausing to swat at a fly with her paw. "We actually had a little debate about it."

"Really?" I know the ladies like to argue about everything. But when it comes to their best friend and the sorry state I'm in, I'd like to think the decision to check on me would be a no-brainer. "Well, I did manage to escape this cone at supper time and then again at bedtime. But sadly, it came back."

Goldie blinks a few times. "We can see that."

"Though actually what's more worrisome at the moment is our precious Angel," Patches says. "She was in such a hurry to get over there this morning, she must've forgotten to bring us along."

"Um, I wouldn't call it forgetting," Goldie says. "She slammed the gate and told us to stay. It's pretty clear she wants to keep us away from you."

"What?! Why?" I whip my cone-head toward the porch. Hattie's wearing that same tall hat and cape. She's holding a little ball and rolling it around in her fingers. Angel flips a small, clear box over and over in her hands.

"Maybe Angel's afraid we're a bad influence on you," Goldie huffs.

"Now, we don't know anything for sure," Patches chimes in. "But Angel did mention your name, Fenway. And come to think of it, she may have waggled a finger when she said it."

Normally, I'd protest. I'd tell the ladies they can't be right. But then I look over at the short humans again. Could keeping me and my friends separated have something to do with the other terrible things that've been going on?

Even if it doesn't, it means more misery. If the ladies can't come over, I can't play. I already can't chase down rodent-y crooks. I can't eat. I can't lick my paw. I can't do anything!

Eventually, the ladies mosey away from the fence. Apparently to have fun without me. I slump down in the grass, watching Hattie and Angel.

They play a game with that tiny ball and box over and over, even though neither of them looks to be enjoying it. And every time Angel drops the ball, Hattie winces and studies the little book with her brow furrowed. She must be concentrating very hard. Or maybe the book has angered her somehow. Angel seems more interested in munching on peanuts.

When the short humans head inside for lunch, I follow them into the Eating Place. Hattie and Angel wolf down delicious-smelling grilled cheese sandwiches and juicy peaches. They chat with Fetch Man and Food Lady, who once again reek of wet paint.

I'm firmly focused on that grilled cheese, but then rustling noises out in the Dog Park steal my attention. And my tail rises in alarm.

I trot over to the door. That thieving chipmunk is headed this way! He scampers up the steps and scurries across the porch like he's not being watched. Doesn't he realize a ferocious dog is right on the other side of the screen?

My fur bristles. I bare my teeth. "Stop, thief!" I bark.

But that criminal-in-stripes keeps on roaming through the porch as if he's not even the least bit threatened. He hops around the Nana-toys, his head twitching from side to side, obviously searching for loot to take.

Thanks to this Cone of Doom, I can only get so close to the screen. I swipe it with my paw, but *ouch!* Stifling a yelp, I turn on a growl. "You've been caught in the act, robber!" I bark. "You'll never get away with it!"

He really must not be able to hear, because he continues casing the porch for the heist. He circles the fake flowers, darts around the metal rings, then pounces on a peanut shell. I bark ferociously as he pecks and pecks, his cheeks ballooning with hot property.

"FEN-way!" Hattie snaps. She pulls me away from the door like I'm the one who committed a crime.

That thieving chipmunk might've won another round. But he'd better watch his back. Because if he thinks I'm going to give up because of a Cone of Doom, he's totally nuts!

The humans finish eating, and instead of trudging upstairs toward that stinky paint, Food Lady and Fetch Man come outside with us. I get the feeling something is about to happen because they are full of anticipation. I watch them set up chairs in the grass, facing the porch. Then they plop down, chatting happily and waiting, with curious expressions.

Hattie and Angel fiddle with the Nana-toys on the porch. Hattie sweeps into the flouncy cape and plunks the tall hat on her head. As Angel sets the toys on top of the Nana-box, Hattie ducks back inside the house. But she doesn't go anywhere. She just stands on the other side of the door like she's waiting for something, too. Or hiding.

I start limping up to the door to check it out when Fetch Man calls out, "Here, Fenway!" and my cone-head turns. Fetch Man slaps his leg, his eyes sparkling.

Yippee! I know that look! Does he have a stick to throw? My tail wagging, I stumble down the porch steps—*ow!* My white paw is throbbing. And when did it get so big and puffy?

By the time I've hobbled over to Fetch Man, he's apparently forgotten all about playing fetch and that's fine with me. I have a painful paw to lick!

I sink down beside Fetch Man, twisting my neck and batting the cone. I have to reach that paw! But no matter how hard I try, it's not enough. All I manage to do is tire myself out.

I stop for a rest, and just in time. It sounds like we're about to find out what's happening. Angel sashays across the porch, her arms gesturing toward the door. "Hattie-the-Grrate!" she cries.

Hattie saunters out, her cape fluttering behind her like wings. Angel rushes up to her, an excited look on her face. She extends her arms at Hattie and shouts, "Ta-da!"

Hattie smiles weakly and takes a bow. Even from down here in the grass, I can smell how nervous she is.

Fetch Man and Food Lady whistle and clap, full of enthusiasm. Hattie responds by wringing her hands and fidgeting.

I'm almost afraid to find out what she's up to. But I sit up tall, determined not to miss a trick, even though my paw is throbbing.

Hattie hovers over the Nana-box like it's a table. She grabs the clear plastic box, its lid, and the tiny ball and offers them to Angel.

Angel examines the little box and ball like she's never seen them before, even though she spent the whole morning playing with them. She pokes a finger inside the box as if to show everyone how empty it is.

Angel passes the toys back to Hattie.

Hattie places the ball inside the box. *Clunk!* She gives Angel the lid.

While all eyes are on Angel studying the lid, Hattie fiddles with the box. Appearing satisfied, Angel hands it back to Hattie. Hattie plunks the lid onto the top of the box and quickly drapes a cloth over it. She waves the skinny stick through the air. "Abracadabra!" she says.

Fetch Man and Food Lady hold their breath, like they're expecting something to happen. Hattie sets the abracadabra stick down. She pulls off the cloth and stuffs it in her pocket.

The clear plastic box is empty again. In unison,

the tall humans gasp. Angel joins them, clapping and cheering. Food Lady stomps her feet. "Brah-voh!" Fetch Man yells.

Hattie grins. She holds the box up as if to demonstrate exactly how empty it is.

My cone-head swivels from Angel to Food Lady to Fetch Man. They look puzzled, like they don't know where that tiny ball went. But at the same time, they're acting thrilled, like something spectacular just happened.

It's almost like they think the ball just disappeared. Are they really that gullible?

Hattie takes a bow. A deep one this time. The others keep on clapping and clapping. "Hattie-the-Grrate!" Angel calls.

Is it possible that none of them knows what happened to the ball? It's right there in Hattie's pocket. Why aren't they at least looking for it?

One thing's for sure—something strange is going on. Maybe my humans can't smell the ball. Maybe they need a Jack Russell Terrier to save the day. I do know a few things about fetching balls.

I limp up the porch steps on three legs, my sore white paw curled under my chest. I can't let throbbing pain stop me.

I hop over and leap on Hattie. My white paw is puffy

and hurting, but it can still claw Hattie's pocket. Where the ball and cloth are hiding.

"FEN-way!" Hattie yells, brushing me off. She sounds annoyed.

"What? I'm only trying to show everybody where the ball—yooooow!" I frantically wave my paw, hopping around Hattie. "It's on fire again! My paw is back on fire!"

Hattie shrieks and scoops me up. "Fenway!" she cries, staring at my paw. Her eyes are surprised and panicked.

Suddenly, I'm surrounded. The humans are all talking at once. They smell worried. And there's another smell, too. *Sniff . . . sniff . . .* Sour garbage? Rotting meat?

The odor is coming from my fiery paw. And no matter how far I stretch, I cannot lick it.

As Hattie hugs me tight, I can almost see it over the edge of the cone. Whoa! Is it ever puffy!

Next thing I know, me and Hattie are in the back seat of the car. And we're zooming out of the driveway.

CHAPTER 12

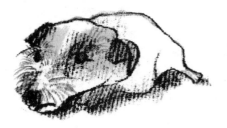

The trip is frantic. I squirm and twist every way I can, my neck stretching, my tongue thrusting and reaching. I need to lick that puffy white paw! But I can't get to it no matter what I do. I have to keep trying. I must have relief!

Hattie rocks me. She sings to me. She whispers in a gentle voice. Does she think this is snuggle time and nothing is wrong?

It's great that she's so devoted to me. But if she really wanted to help, she'd take this Cone of Doom off my head again. "Hattie, can't you see? Everything is wrong!" I whimper and thrash in her arms. "My paw's on fire! I must lick the puffiness that smells sour and rotten!"

"Shhh," she murmurs, stroking my back. Is that supposed to make me feel better?

I won't stop protesting until she gets the message. I'm struggling and whining as the car stops and goes quiet. Hattie carries me out of the car. My tail wags hopefully. Are we headed someplace wonderful and soothing?

We follow Fetch Man into a building that looks awfully familiar. My tail sags with a terrible memory. We enter an open space lined with chairs. It smells like dogs and cats and bunnies and birds. And also like misery and fear.

It's so horribly familiar. Like a nightmare, only real.

Fetch Man goes to the counter and speaks to a lady human.

Me and Hattie lag behind. "Shhh," she murmurs, even though I'm not making any noise.

I consider my options, but there's only one thing to do—make a run for it! In a flash, I spring out of her arms and onto the cold, hard floor. *Ouch!* I bolt toward the door, or at least I do the best I can on three legs.

"Fenway!" Hattie rushes after me, but I'm already halfway there. I have to get away. No way am I going back to the torture chamber with pokes and pricks. And the Table of Panic!

Hopping as fast as I can, I'm almost to the door. It's closed, but I can smell freedom on the other side.

"Fenway, come!" Hattie swoops me into her arms as I kick in protest. "No-no-no!" she coos, like "no" is the Sweetest Word Ever.

I keep on kicking. "You obviously don't remember, Hattie," I bark. "But this place is bad news. We've got to get out of here!"

She looks at me with a pained face, like maybe she's beginning to get it. But right then, we're interrupted by a howling that can only be described as dreadful. We turn toward a white Husky who's slumped around her human's feet.

"Oooooh," she howls, her eyes drooping with sadness. "I'm sooooo miserable."

"I am, tooooo," a huge black dog chimes in in less-than-perfect harmony. He looks like a cross between a Rottweiler and a Lab. And his face is the picture of gloom. "I want to get out of heeeeere."

"Rrrrraaaaarrrrr!" A painful meow spews from a carrier on an old lady's lap. And then, "Hsssss!" As if the already-depressing melody could get any more grating.

My ears wilt in sympathy. I wiggle. I kick. "Listen, Hattie, it's unanimous. We need to ditch this place!"

But all she does is rub my back some more, like that's somehow helping.

"Okay, Fenway." The lady from behind the counter

ushers me and Hattie and Fetch Man into a tiny room and closes the door.

Uh-oh.

The odor hits me first—terror and agony. I zoom in on the wall and the Table of Panic. I remember scraping claws, sliding paws. I start trembling with dread.

Fetch Man gives Hattie a look of reassurance. He pats her shoulder like she's the one who's horrified.

"Aw, Fenway," Hattie sings. She dances and sways. "It's okay . . ."

I nuzzle into her shirt, the Cone of Doom resting in the crook of her elbow. Maybe she's not getting my need to escape or lick my paw, but at least one thing is clear—Hattie is overflowing with devotion. She's always on my side, especially now. All she wants to do is shower me with extra love and attention.

Paw or no paw, cone or no cone, all that matters is Hattie's love for me. When she's got my back, I can handle anything.

The side door opens and a lady walks in. She's wearing a white coat. Dark hair's piled loosely on top of her head. She smiles with wide, kind eyes. "Fenway?" she says.

I respond by shaking.

Because she's moving toward me. She's looking me in the eyes. And her breath smells spicy, like cinnamon.

I know this lady. I faced her before. And I did not win.

I squirm with new urgency. "Hurry, Hattie! Before it's too late!"

Hattie stays put. She rocks me some more, like it's just the two of us, upstairs in her bed, and Spicy Breath isn't there.

Except she is here. My mortal enemy is mere steps away. She's hovering like a scary dark cloud. Are loud boom-kabooms coming next? Or something even worse?

I whip my cone-head from side to side. "Help, Hattie! Help!" I have to make her realize how terribly I'm suffering, how much I need her. It worked before. It has to work now!

"What are you waiting for?" I bark. Spicy Breath is reaching for me! "There's no time to lose! We have to make a run for it like RIGHT NOW!"

I feel Hattie's weight shifting, her arms moving. Something's happening. Is she headed for the door? Are we about to make our escape?

I lift my head. The Cone of Doom tilts and wobbles to one side, just in time for me to see . . .

Spicy Breath's face! Her wide eyes are peering down at me!

"Hattie! Hattie!" I yelp, thrashing and kicking hysterically. "Let's gooooo!"

But instead of going, Hattie stays where she is. And even worse, I feel two other hands close around me.

I jerk and jolt and kick with all my might. "Get your paws off me, lady! Or you'll be sorry!"

One pair of hands releases its grip. I turn my cone-head toward Hattie, desperately hoping that she's the one still holding me. But the sorry look in her eyes tells me I'm wrong. My heart smashes to pieces.

I'm in the hands of the enemy. Why didn't Hattie save me?

I look back at her. "How could you do this to me, Hattie?"

She drops her gaze like she can't bear to look at me.

I know how she feels.

Spicy Breath lowers me onto the Table of Panic. She clutches me tight. Fetch Man stands on my other side, leaning in. I'm trapped.

R-r-r-r-rip! The Cone of Doom falls off my head.

WOWEE! I did not see *that* coming! I shake and shake, cool air rushing through my fur. What a refreshing feeling! I glance around the room, almost happy.

But one second later, I realize that while the cone may be off, everything else is terrible. Spicy Breath seizes me again. Fetch Man bends over, gripping my hind legs. And my white paw is still on fire and throbbing, and I still can't lick it!

Then, out of nowhere, a sharp odor burns in my nostrils. Eeeee-yew! It smells like the spray bottle that Food Lady uses in the kitchen. I whip my snout from side to side trying to get away from that obnoxious scent.

Spicy Breath holds my front leg. Owwwww! A wet cloth wipes my fiery paw. I pull and pull, but Spicy Breath and Fetch Man are on me and I can't even budge. Where is Hattie? Why isn't she helping me?

I know why. My whole body sinks with the sickening realization—Hattie's the one who handed me over.

My own short human. The girl I swore to love and protect. The one I'm always on guard for. The one I fight battles for every day. She let me down.

I shudder with the horrible truth.

Spicy Breath talks to Fetch Man and Hattie in a gentle yet bossy voice. "In-fect-id," she says. Whatever that means.

"Soke-it," she commands. She takes a carton out of a cabinet and hands it to them. It looks like milk, only it didn't come from the tall frosty box where hot dogs and mayonnaise live.

Fetch Man gazes at Hattie, one eyebrow raised.

"Okay," she says.

Spicy Breath wipes my paw some more with that stinky cloth.

"Owwwww!" I yelp. It's all too clear—this battle is over. And I've lost.

"Look," Spicy Breath says. She opens a little plastic bottle. Out rattles a tiny morsel that doesn't smell anything like a treat. Or a peanut. She shows it to Fetch Man and Hattie.

Spicy Breath tilts my head up to the ceiling. She obviously wants us all to look. What's so interesting up there? All I see is a plain, boring ceiling.

I continue searching, when suddenly my jaws are pried open and a tasteless morsel drops in. Before I can even gag. Spicy Breath's hand clamps my jaws shut. Fingers caress my throat in downward strokes that are anything but soothing.

As soon as I swallow, my jaw releases. I'm about to growl, but—what's this? Spicy Breath is holding a treat!

"Give me that!" I bark.

It works! She tosses it into my mouth. *Chomp!* Mmmmm, yummy! "More, please!"

As I swallow again, Spicy Breath smiles. "See?" she asks Fetch Man and Hattie.

Hattie nods in agreement. Or approval. Is she surprised that I can stand up for myself?

Spicy Breath twists the cap off a tube that looks like toothpaste. She grabs my white paw and smears creamy goo on the bottom. "Ow! Cut that out!" I bark, recoiling. "Or else!"

She backs away. I puff out my chest. Apparently, I can still be intimidating when I put my mind to it!

The humans focus on Spicy Breath as she talks and talks and talks. She scribbles for a moment, then thrusts a piece of paper at Fetch Man with a very serious look.

Something changes, though I'm not sure what. Fetch Man and Hattie exchange concerned looks. Wiping a tear, Hattie nods with determination.

Everybody's still alarmed, yet calmer somehow.

Including me. When Fetch Man releases my hind legs, Spicy Breath backs even farther away. Best of all, the Cone of Doom is gone. There's just a curved sheet of plastic lying on the counter.

But it's probably going to reappear when I least expect it. No point in taking chances. "Stay away from me, Cone of Doom!" I bark. "If I never see you again, it will be too soon!"

"Shhh," Hattie murmurs as Spicy Breath begins talking some more.

My white paw is still puffy and hurting. The Cone of Doom has been defeated. And the humans are clearly distracted by Spicy Breath. This can only mean one thing—Opportunity. I drop down on the Table of Panic for a good, long lick.

Slurp . . . slurp . . . slurp . . . eeeeewwwww! *Paaaaa-tooey!* My paw tastes awful—bitter, like lemons! *Paaaaatooey! Paaaaatooey! Paaaaatooey!*

"Aw, Fenway," Hattie coos sadly, stroking my neck.

I gag some more, but the horrible taste is still there.

Hattie nuzzles my ear. "Sorry," she whispers.

I turn away. Me too.

@Hapter 13

Back in the car, I'm curled up near one
window, and Hattie's strapped in beside the other.

She can't take her sad eyes off me. Clearly, she feels
bad about what happened. She's liable to let me get away
with anything right now—chewing the upholstery,
bounding into the front seat with Fetch Man, searching for snacks in her bag.

The trouble is, I don't want to do any of those things.
All I want to do is lick away my paw's awful soreness.
But I can't put my tongue on something that tastes so
bitter! Talk about an obstacle!

I need to find a way around it. Hattie hates seeing me
suffer, like Goldie and Patches said. Somehow I need to

use this to my advantage. After all, I'm all about pouncing on Opportunity.

By the time the car goes quiet in the garage, I'm determined to turn things around. Hattie carries me out of the car and into the Eating Place. I give myself a vigorous shake. At least that Cone of Doom has disappeared. Hopefully for good!

Food Lady glances up from the counter. She's still dressed in raggedy clothes and reeks of wet paint. Fetch Man must not mind the odor because he breezes over and kisses her cheek.

Hattie chatters at her, apparently explaining what happened, because all eyes are focused on me. Food Lady looks surprised. Did she not expect me to trounce the cone?

Fetch Man pats Hattie's shoulder, then sets the carton, tube, and little rattle-y bottle on the table. He reaches into his pocket and unfolds a piece of paper. He stares at it, speaking in a serious tone.

Hattie nods, full of determination, and strokes my head. My family's paying way too much attention to me. They're obviously up to something. And from the intense looks on their faces, it's not playing with toys or fetching balls out in the Dog Park.

Hattie nuzzles my ears. "Soke-it," she says. She must

be apologizing again, because she smells sad and her voice sounds like a promise.

Does this mean everything will be better from now on?

"Thanks," I bark, licking her cheek. "I'll take it."

With the carton hooked on one finger, Hattie carries me out of the Eating Place, down the hallway, and into the Washing Room. My fur prickles. Oh no! This is not a good sign!

I squirm desperately. "Let's go someplace else," I bark. "Like the Dog Park?"

"Shhh," Hattie murmurs, calm as can be.

As if there's anything to feel calm about. "Bad news, Hattie! It's called the Washing Room for a reason! Can't we go play outside?"

She acts like she either doesn't get it or doesn't care. She puts the carton on the counter and opens it.

Normally, I'd trust that any carton or box or package that Hattie opens is something wonderful, like a snack. But right now, my guard is up. And with good reason. Hattie's motives are clearly suspect. Snacks do not belong in the Washing Room. This carton doesn't smell like any snack I've ever smelled before. It smells like Spicy Breath.

I kick more vigorously. "Put me down!" I bark. "You can't fool me. I know you're up to no good."

"Shhh . . . shhh . . ." she murmurs again. Her grip on me tightens even more and water starts whooshing into the sink.

Another bad sign. When water whooshes into the sink, Hattie usually stands over it rubbing her hands or brushing her teeth while I wait safely on the floor or out in the hallway. Right now, none of those things is happening.

She's got a plan. Clearly, it involves that water. And me.

My fur ripples in panic. "Please, no!" I wriggle. I thrash. I'm desperate to get loose. "I'm not even dirty!"

The whooshing continues. The water level rises higher and higher. Hattie's obviously planning to torture me with that water, no matter how badly I try to convince her otherwise.

I keep up the squirming and wiggling anyway. "What did I ever do to deserve this?" I yelp.

My protesting must finally be getting through to her, because Hattie touches the faucet and the rushing water stops. Whew! That was a lot of hard work. Now if only I could convince her to loosen her grip, too, I could bolt on out of here.

But she's got me good and tight. As much as I kick and twist, I can't move a single inch.

Hattie tips the carton and pours glittery crystals into the water. They look like the sugar that Food Lady sprinkles on cookies. But they smell like salt. Talk about curious. Are we going to drink it? Is it some kind of game?

"Let's go, Fenway," she coaxes sweetly.

Does she know something I don't? Is there something very interesting about this water?

I lean over for a better look, and then—*Plop! Splash!*

What the—? My paws churn and thrash in the warm, salty water. My whole coat is soaked through. No—not a bath! I hate baths!

Hattie wipes a strand of wet hair from her eyes. "Stop, Fenway!" She grabs my white paw and tries to dunk it. Apparently, it's the only part of me she wants to bathe. But all of me is wet, wet, wet!

I twist my paw away from her. "Let me go!" I yelp, my hind legs scrambling. I'm slipping and sliding. Water sloshes everywhere. Hattie's hair and clothes are as wet as I am.

"FEN-way!" Hattie jumps back, pulling on her soaked shirt. Obviously distracted, she releases her grip.

Ha! My big chance! I spring onto the edge of the sink and vault onto the counter. I'm about to leap off, when I pull up short. Uh-oh. The floor is a long way down.

"Fenway!" Hattie cries, reaching for me.

But I'm too quick. I leap onto the lid of the deep, gurgling bowl. My paws skid, and I nearly crash into the wall.

Hattie lunges as I land on the mat. I'm almost to the door when a higher priority calls.

I pause to give myself a good shake. It starts at my nose, twists through my body, and ends at my tail. Water sprays all over the cabinet, the mat, and Hattie's legs.

"Fenway!" she calls. "Stop!" She goes to grab me, but I'm already out the door. I hear her slip and stumble on the wet floor before she heads into the hallway after me.

I hop and hobble down the hall, making a wide turn at the Eating Place. It's clear that Hattie wants to catch me and put me back in that sink. There's no way that's going to happen.

I dive under a chair and curl into a ball. Maybe she won't spot me.

"Fenway!" I hear footsteps race in. With a loud sigh, Hattie goes to the counter. Has she given up? Did she realize the water was a big mistake and now we're going to have buttery vanilla cookies?

My tail thumps with hope. But in the meantime, I've got a sore paw to lick. *Slurp ... slurp ... slurp ...*

Aaaaah! Sweet relief! It's a bit salty, but the good news is it doesn't taste yucky or bitter. *Slurp . . . slurp*—ouch!

Hattie's on the floor next to me, my white paw in her hands. And no trace of vanilla cookies. Or snacks of any kind.

"Give me my paw back!" I bark, tugging and tugging. "I wasn't finished licking yet!"

Hattie squeezes the tube, and creamy goo squirts onto my paw. She smears it around.

"What do you think you're doing?" I whine. "Cut that out!"

Ha! She gets the message and lets go. Did she decide to quit? Or was I that persuasive?

Whatever the reason, I have to get back to work. *Slurp . . . slurp . . . slurp . . .* eeeeewwwww! *Paaaaatooey!*

That horrible taste is back—bitter, bitter, bitter! *Paaaaatooey! Paaaaatooey! Paaaaatooey!*

As I gag, Hattie wags her finger at me. Her face looks strangely satisfied.

I recoil in sadness. It makes no sense. Hattie spread that goo on my paw, and now it tastes terrible. And she seems pleased that I can't lick it. Doesn't she want my paw to get better?

"Hattie?" Angel's voice floats through the back door.

"Hey." Hattie springs up and rushes over.

I creep out from under the chair and crane my neck.

The short humans chatter through the screen. Angel taps the side of the door with a stick. The abracadabra stick? "C'mon," she says.

While Angel is talking, Hattie sneaks a few glances at me. Like she can't decide which one of us to pay attention to.

I have a feeling she's going to choose me. And for once, I'm not sure if that's good news.

CHAPTER 14

Hattie raises a finger at Angel and then turns around. She crouches low and slaps her knee. "Fenn-waay," she calls, all cheery, like we're going out to play, same as always. Could it be true?

I burrow farther back.

She strides over, her grin impossibly wide. "Here, Fenway!"

I let her swoop me up, even though every hair on my back is telling me not to.

"Let's go." She slides the door open, and we step onto the porch. Angel is waiting with the abracadabra stick.

I squint into the sunshine and survey the Dog Park. A butterfly flutters through the zucchini plants in the vegetable patch. A light breeze ripples the leaves in the giant tree. The bushes are quiet. But a rodent-y smell is everywhere.

Clearly, that thieving chipmunk is hiding out nearby.

What other crimes is he conjuring up? He appears and disappears when I least expect it. He stole those peanuts right under my nose. Who knows what else he's capable of?

I have to stay on guard. That villain could pop up at any moment.

Hattie sets me down, staring at me like she's afraid to look away. "Stay," she says, pointing at me.

My tail droops. Staying still on the porch is not what I expected we'd be doing. But maybe it's better than the sink and all that splashing water.

Angel goes to the Nana-box. She fishes out the black cape, the tall hat, and a couple of toys. She lays them out on the table the way Food Lady sets out supper.

Hattie steals a quick peek at the Nana-box, then back at me. For a second, I worry that she might stuff me in that scary box again. But she doesn't appear to be in any hurry to get over there. I'd almost feel relieved, except the way she keeps focusing on me is kind of bad, too. Is she considering an even scarier plan? I thought things were getting better.

"Come on, Hattie," Angel says, waving the abraca-dabra stick.

Hattie puts her hands on her hips. Her eyes narrow at me. Her expression is stern, but at the same time her brow is scrunched up like she's worried. "Stay," she commands.

Like I've moved!

Hattie joins Angel at the Nana-box. She wraps herself in the black cape. She plops the tall hat on her head. She grabs the abracadabra stick. Pausing, she gazes over at me, a satisfied look spreading across her face. Is she glad that I haven't disappeared?

Angel munches on peanuts. Hattie takes the lid on and off the clear little box. She seems intent on playing with it, though she glances in my direction every now and then.

I'm sprawled on my belly, forepaws out in front of me, trying not to worry. And keeping my eye out for that chipmunk.

Hattie's trying to pay attention to the toys, but she's obviously distracted. Angel must notice because she taps Hattie's shoulder a bunch of times. "C'mon," she says, her voice impatient.

Hattie plunks the ball into the clear box. She covers it with the cloth and gives it a tap. "Abracadabra," she says.

After pausing a moment, she pulls the cloth away, and the little ball falls on the floor.

Angel's face falls, like the ball was the last thing she

wanted to see. Was she expecting it to be in Hattie's pocket like it was the last time?

Hattie whooshes out a breath and plucks the ball off the floor. She drops it inside the box and drapes the cloth over it. "Abracadabra!" she cries, smacking it with the stick. She takes a long time pulling the cloth away, and the ball falls onto the floor again. She slams the box down on the table, like she's mad at it. What'd it ever do to her?

"It's okay," Angel says in a soothing voice, picking up the ball. Hattie sinks into a chair. Her head hanging, she's the picture of disappointment. And frustration.

It's pretty obvious that whatever she's trying to do isn't working. And from the way she's looking over at me all the time, it's also pretty obvious she's more concerned about watching me than playing with those toys.

A fly buzzes around my ear, and I swipe it away. My ear perks right back up. Is that a snapping sound coming from the bushes?

Turning, all I see are bushy branches. I push myself up and glance at Hattie. She's chattering away with Angel, her forehead in her hands. "Fenway," she mutters.

She's saying my name, but she's focused on Angel. I turn back toward the snapping sound.

Over in the bushes, a low branch sways and *pow!* A stripe-y chipmunk shoots across the grass!

My hackles stiffen. I have to chase him. I have to warn him to get lost. It's my job to patrol the Dog Park.

My paw hurts so much. But I can't let that stop me. Duty calls!

I'm about to limp to the steps when that thieving chipmunk makes a turn. He's heading right for the porch.

I creep back, my fur bristling with bravery. "Stop where you are, you scoundrel!" I bark. "This porch is off-limits!"

He scurries as far as the bottom step, then abruptly halts. His tiny nose twitches. His head bobs from side to side like he's searching for something.

Probably more goods to steal!

Assuming attack posture, I give him my best snarl. "Beat it!" I bark. "You don't belong here!"

The thieving chipmunk doesn't come any closer. But he doesn't flee, either. He just stays put, then starts rummaging in the grass.

I open my mouth and am about to give him another warning when he pops back up. His paws are clutching a whole peanut shell. He stuffs it in one side of his face, then picks up another. He stuffs that one in, too, and his cheeks are bulging like balloons. What a weird trick!

In a flash, he pivots and flies back toward the bushes.

I hobble to the top step. "Drop that peanut!" I bark helplessly. He dives under the lowest branch and disappears. Again.

There's no sense chasing him now. But maybe I could inspect the bushes. Could there be something in there I haven't noticed before?

I look back at Hattie. She's still chattering with Angel, who offers her a peanut. Hattie unpeels it, saying my name. She also says "in-feck-tid," and "soke-it." She sounds frustrated. What could it mean?

Maybe it's not important. What *is* important is that her head's turned toward Angel. And away from me. She's the very definition of preoccupied.

I could pad over and check out the bushes before she even notices I'm gone.

I inch to the edge of the porch and stumble down the steps. As soon as my paws hit the grass, I hear jingling in the Dog Park next door.

I hobble over to the Friend Gate for a look. Through the slats, I see two black noses. "Is that you, ladies?"

"Fenway?" Patches calls in her lovely voice.

"I hardly recognized you without that cone," Goldie says with genuine surprise.

"Well, that's the good news, I guess," I say.

Goldie cocks her head. "You guess?"

I sigh. "It's hard to see any good at all in what happened."

Patches gazes at me with kind eyes. "Oh, you poor dear. Do tell us. That's what friends are for."

I barely know where to begin. But then I look into Patches's sympathetic face, and the words begin flowing out of my mouth. "Remember when I asked about your humans standing by and letting you get tortured? When you went to that place with the—" I stop and shiver. "*Clippers?*"

Goldie paws the ground as if to show off her short claws. "How could we forget?"

"You didn't go to the groomer's!" Patches says, her face clearly horrified at the thought. Or maybe she's just surprised because I look as ragged as always.

"No! It was that awful place again with the grabbing and poking and the Spicy Breath lady," I say, barely able to make eye contact. "And my Hattie—my beloved Hattie—she—she . . ." I can't even speak.

"Oh, Fenway," Patches says. "Did she stand by while something terrible happened?"

"Worse!" I practically spit. "She handed me over. Again!"

Goldie startles. "You mean she did this before?"

"No—yes—I don't know," I wail. "But she feels

really bad about it. She promised everything will get better."

Patches blinks. "Are you sure?"

Goldie shakes her head like she can't believe her ears. "Seriously?"

"Well, she sounded awfully sad. And sorry, too," I say, slumping down in the grass. "But since then, she splashed me with water and she smeared yucky goo on my paw. It's all so confusing."

The ladies exchange a worried glance.

"So you thought things were improving, but then they got worse?" Patches says.

"What are you going to do?" Goldie asks.

I shake my head. "I wish I knew."

I glance over at the porch. Hattie springs up. Her face is excited, like she just got an idea. "Pool!" she cries.

Goldie clears her throat. "Well, I think you're about to find out."

CHAPTER 15

I get out of the way just in time. Angel comes barreling by and disappears through the Friend Gate.

"Fenway!" Hattie calls, clapping her hands.

Through the fence, I see Angel streaking across the Dog Park next door. The ladies turn to follow. "What's going on?" I ask.

Patches looks over her shoulder. "We'll let you know."

"Fenway!" Hattie calls again. She rushes up and whisks me into her arms. I guess I'll have to find out later on.

Hattie races to the porch and slides the door open.

Food Lady and Fetch Man are in the Eating Place, standing at the counter. They are sipping steaming cups that smell like coffee even though morning was a Long Time Ago. Fetch Man's shirt is splattered with paint. Food Lady fights back a yawn. Both of their faces look tired.

Fetch Man glances up as we breeze by. "Howz-Fenway?" he asks.

Hattie clutches me in her arms. "Okay," she says, in a voice more confident than I've heard in a while. We rush upstairs past the horrible paint smell and fly into her room.

She sets me on the bed and rips off her clothes. Oh no! Are we headed to the Bathtub Room for more splashing? I paw through the rumpled blankets, preparing to hide. And grab the used-to-be bear.

But then, out of the corner of my eye, I see a promising sign. Hattie is pulling on her swimsuit.

My tail wags with curiosity. Is something wonderful about to happen? Are we going to the pond for a picnic?

Before I have time to figure it out, Hattie scoops me back up and races downstairs. My fur bristles as we pop into the Washing Room, but luckily all she does is grab a towel and that same carton from before, then dash back down the hall.

As we pass by the Eating Place, Fetch Man and Food

Lady look up with arching eyebrows, like they have no idea what's going on. I begin to worry. If we're going to the pond, shouldn't they be getting in the car?

Hattie calls out, "soke-it!" and "pool," then hurries to the back door. We step onto the porch right as Angel bursts through the Friend Gate again, carrying what looks like a giant supper dish. Except it's bendy and has nothing in it. "Got-it!" she cries.

Hattie pumps her fist. "Yes!" She sets me down and heads to the side gate, stopping at the coiled-up hose. She beckons Angel over.

I follow along, my nose pulsing with wonder. And suspicion. The giant water dish smells like plastic and cobwebs and garage. But also a little bit like dog. *Sniff . . . sniff . . .* Goldie? And Patches? The scents are so faint, I can't be sure.

Is this their water dish? It's awfully big. But then again, there are two of them. And they're both a lot bigger than me. Do they really get *that* thirsty?

Angel drops the dish in the grass while Hattie picks up the end of the hose. She lays it in the dish, and water starts rushing out.

The short humans chatter, and I hear my name a couple of times. I get the feeling this giant water dish is for me. But why? I already have a water dish in the

Eating Place. And besides that, this one is so big and its sides are so high, it'd be hard for me to take a drink without falling in . . .

Uh-oh. I start to get a bad feeling. I hobble over to the Friend Gate and peer through the slats. The ladies' noses greet me.

"How lovely is this?" Patches says, her eyes bright and happy. "I haven't seen that old thing in ages. It's been tucked in the garage behind Angel's sled and her rain boots for as long as I can remember."

"It would be lovely if *we* were using it." Goldie's face is scrunched. "Why'd Angel bring our wading pool over there?"

"Wading pool?" I say, glancing back at Hattie and Angel. "Isn't that your giant water dish?"

"Well, we certainly did drink from it," Patches says.

"Maybe you did," Goldie says. "But I mostly lounged around in it."

Patches sighs. "It was so refreshing. Especially on a hot day like today."

"Ladies," I say, the picture becoming clearer in my mind. "Are you saying your short human plopped you into the water? Like a . . . b-b-bath?"

"Not exactly," Patches says.

Goldie drops down for a quick scratch as if she's not concerned at all. "It was more like we climbed in."

My fur prickles. "You mean on purpose?"

"Of course," Patches says. "Splashing in the wading pool is fun, Fenway. You should give it a try."

I gaze over at the pool. Hattie is pouring the salty crystals into the water. She stirs it around with her hand. I shudder. It's way too much like what happened in the sink.

I turn back to the ladies. "Maybe you think the wading pool is fun, but I have a feeling something bad is going to happen."

"Normally I'd disagree," Goldie says. "But given all the unpleasant things you've endured lately, you might be right."

"Goldie!" Patches says sharply. "We don't know anything for sure."

Goldie sneers. "Haven't you been listening? And watching?"

"I know!" I say, bouncing and curling my white paw. "I have to be ready to protect myself."

"Well, get ready," Patches says, and I turn around.

Hattie is sprinting toward me. She's smiling, but her eyes are all business. A suspicious combination.

"Gotta go," I say to the ladies, limping off. But there's no way I can outrun her. I'm barely a few steps away when Hattie lifts me into her arms.

I kick feverishly. "Put me down!"

Full of determination, Hattie strides back to the wading pool where Angel is waiting. It's halfway filled with water. I writhe and twist and do everything I can to convince Hattie to let me go.

Except nothing works. The more I revolt, the more her grip tightens. I brace myself for what's coming— she's going to plunk me into that water! I squeeze my eyes shut . . .

But I'm not plunking down. And I'm not in the water. Hattie's still holding me tight. Did my protests finally get through to her? Is that too much to hope for?

Probably. As I open my eyes, Hattie steps over the edge of the wading pool herself and plops down. With me in her lap!

Splash!

Nooooo! Lukewarm water seeps into my fur. It smells salty. And worst of all, it feels *wet*! Just like a bath!

My paws churn the water, splashing and sending rippling waves over the edge of the pool. But as hard as I paddle, I'm not getting away. I just keep on getting wetter and wetter. Why is this happening? She knows how much I hate baths. "What's the big idea, Hattie?" I yelp. "I'm not even dirty!"

"Shhh, Fenway," she murmurs, her voice soothing, like she's not tormenting me or anything. Hattie grabs my front leg and dunks my white paw in the water.

"NO!" I bark, wiggling and squirming. I have to convince her to give up this madness. I kick and kick. "Let me out of here!"

"Ow! Ow!" Hattie cries, rubbing her skin where scratches are appearing. She's distracted all right. But unfortunately, she's still got my front leg underwater. And she won't let go.

As if this whole experience isn't horrible enough, right then a nasty squirrel scampers by. He glares at me with beady eyes, flouncing his fluffy tail, and all I can do is watch. "It's an emergency, Hattie! I need to get out of this terrible wa-a-a-a-ater!" I howl.

We both twist and turn, water splashing and sloshing out onto the grass. And through it all, Hattie never releases my white paw. She keeps it completely submerged as if getting it as wet as possible is the entire goal.

I can't rest. I work as hard as I can, flailing and kicking, for all the good it's doing. I'm completely soaked. And to make matters worse, Angel leans over the side of the pool, offering Hattie praise and encouragement. Like that's what she needs!

The more I thrash, the wetter I get. It's the very definition of a sinking strategy.

Clearly, Hattie's winning and I'm losing.

"Poor guy," I hear Patches mutter.

"Wish I had his energy," Goldie says.

Great! The ladies are watching. Like this pathetic scene isn't bad enough on its own. It has to be humiliating, too.

After a Very Long Time and lots more wrestling, me and Hattie climb out of the pool. The breeze ruffles my sopping wet fur, cold as ice. I try to twist and shake, but she's clutching me so tightly, I can hardly move.

Angel drapes a towel around us, and Hattie starts rubbing. Normally, towel rubs are fun and cozy, but this one is a horrible reminder of the torture I've just endured.

Once Hattie finally puts me down and I've enjoyed a series of shakes, I gaze up at her. How did this happen? Weren't we happy? Didn't we mean everything to each other?

The bitter goo gets smeared on my paw again. As Hattie dries herself off and Angel empties the wading pool, I start to worry that the worst may be yet to come.

CHapter 16

My eyelids flutter open. Morning sun pours into Hattie's room. A wide patch of light shines on her bed. Where she is still snoozing peacefully.

I'm on the floor, curled up under the chair. Where I have been for the past two nights, all alone.

It's not nearly as comfy and cozy as Hattie's rumpled blankets that smell like mint and vanilla. But it's far enough away to stay safe. And close enough to keep an eye on her.

I'm better off down here even if it's lonely by myself. Just when I need him most, the used-to-be bear has vanished.

The last two bedtimes, Hattie tried to coax me onto

the bed. But I knew better. She only wanted me close so she could play more tricks on me.

Which is pretty much all she's been doing the past couple of days. Right when I thought things were about to get better!

Even though I've chewed the edge of the wading pool, knocked over the carton of salt, and scratched a lot, Hattie's still managed to torment me with that horrible pool-bath a bunch more times. She was clearly determined to hold me down and dunk my white paw no matter how hard I kicked, splashed, or yelped in protest. Each time was wetter, saltier, and more terrible than the last. In every possible way!

And if the pool-baths weren't bad enough, Hattie rubbed that yucky-tasting goo on my paw every time a bone, squeaky toy, or juicy hot dog just happened to appear and distract me. Talk about devious antics!

More than once I forgot and slurped my paw anyway. *Paaaaatooey!* Every time, it was the Worst Taste Ever! Just thinking about it makes me gag all over again.

And on top of everything else, Hattie's continued to act strangely. Part of her face would go all sweet and loving, while her eyes looked nervous and shifty. Or worried.

She'd lift up my head, just like Spicy Breath did. Then she'd pry my jaws open and quick stuff in a pebbly morsel—probably a peanut! And before I could spit it out, she'd massage my throat until I swallowed.

I'd go to gag, but right then a lovely treat would sail into my mouth. Even though I was on my guard, those treats were impossible to resist. And oh, so distracting! By the time I figured the whole thing was probably a trick, the tasty treat was already chomped and swallowed.

Of course, that part wasn't so bad.

But overall, I have to face facts. Up until now, I've always known what to expect—Hattie loving me, playing with me, taking care of me. And here I am, watching her sleep on the pillow that I'm supposed to be sharing, and it's pretty obvious that all I have to look forward to forever are bad surprises.

When Hattie wakes up, she gazes at me with that worried-but-at-the-same-time-smiling look. It's so unnerving.

We head downstairs toward the familiar aroma of coffee. I haven't smelled bacon or sausages or pancakes since Fetch Man and Food Lady started saying, "Nanacoming." Which they repeat at random times throughout the day, often accompanied by fussing and sighs.

When we arrive at the Eating Place, they're rushing around as usual, chattering and moaning like they both have big jobs left to do. My nose is happy that the paint smell has faded, but it sure would be nice to get back to the Good Old Bacon-y Days.

As Hattie grabs a box of cereal, my ears perk up. A loud *vrooooom . . . vrooooom . . .* is drifting in through the front door. And getting louder. It can only be one thing—a Big Truck!

I race-hobble across the house to the door. I peer out the screen just in time to see the menace himself appear and come to a rumbling halt right in front of our walkway.

"Watch out, Evil Truck!" I bark, my fur standing straight up. "There's a vicious Jack Russell Terrier guarding this house!"

Totally scared, the Evil Truck goes quiet. But it doesn't go away. Instead, two tall humans jump out and head toward the house, clearly ignoring the ferocious warning.

"FEN-way!" Hattie yells, grabbing my collar. She smells annoyed. Where did she come from? She's supposed to be in the Eating Place munching her cereal.

I lunge at the door. "I've got this, Hattie! Just let me at 'em!"

But instead of letting me go, Hattie lifts me into her arms. "Shhh," she says.

"What'd you do that for?" I bark. I squirm. I twist. I

must get loose. The sooner, the better! Because the two tall humans are almost here!

I bare my teeth. "Don't even think about approaching this house!"

"Fenn-waay," Hattie soothes. She clutches me to her chest, nuzzling my fur.

Like I can be deterred from my job. I growl at the tall humans. They are big and burly and wearing boots even though it's not raining or cold outside. A highly suspicious sign. "Beat it!" I bark.

Fetch Man and Food Lady come up behind us, smelling excited, like they are happy to see the Evil Truck. What's the matter with them? Don't they recognize danger when it's right in their faces?

Good thing I'm here. "This is your last warning!" I bark, baring my teeth. "Leave now or else!"

"FEN-way," Food Lady snaps.

"Hattie," Fetch Man scolds. He points to the back of the house.

Hattie nods and hurries to the back door.

"How can you do this?" I bark, kicking and twisting. "We're practically under attack!" I catch one of the tall humans exchanging greetings with Fetch Man before Hattie slides the door open and we're outside on the porch.

I cock my head toward the side gate, but I don't hear any signs of struggle. Am I supposed to believe that Fetch Man can handle himself? Even with one hurt paw, I could totally take those guys. I have a family to protect!

And speaking of which, there's another threat I have to worry about. My head swiveling, I survey the Dog Park. The sky is bright and clear, a light breeze fluttering through my whiskers. I look over at the bushes. Are my eyes playing tricks on me again? Or is that a little head poking out from under the low branches?

I'm itching to bolt out of Hattie's arms and inspect it, but right then the Friend Gate creaks and I whip around. Angel romps through, all smiles. She's carrying another bag of peanuts.

Usually, I'd be thrilled to see Angel. Not to mention the ladies. But lately the ladies have been shut in their own Dog Park, so we can't play. And Angel's been no fun at all. Ever since she brought that wading pool over, she's been part of the problem—helping Hattie hold me down in that horribly wet, salty water. Some friend she turned out to be!

Just the sight of her gives me the shakes.

"Angel?" Hattie says. Her voice is wavery, like she's not sure if she should be happy or sad.

At first, I'm worried she's going to fill the wading pool

again, but instead she joins us on the porch. Angel lopes over to the Nana-box and picks up the abracadabra stick. "Come on," she says, peeling the shell and stuffing a peanut into her mouth.

Hattie eyes the Nana-toys, smelling eager yet anxious. As she puts me down, I hear *bang!* coming from the street. A very loud door is slamming! I limp over to the side gate. It's probably that Evil Truck!

"Go away, you monster!" I paw the gate with my brown paw. I have to stop them. They're clearly dangerous!

"FEN-way!" Hattie appears out of nowhere and whisks me away from the side gate.

"Hey!" I wiggle and wiggle. "I have a truck to scare off!"

Angel strides over, the abracadabra stick still in her hand. "Let's go," she says.

Hattie looks torn. Like she wants to play with Angel. But she also wants to keep me from doing my job.

As the short humans start to bicker, I continue snarling and growling at the Evil Truck. "If you know what's good for you, you'll get away now while you still can!"

And then, mid-bark, a Very Big Idea pops into my mind.

Chapter 17

I look for my chance all afternoon. But Hattie is on me like fur. If I didn't know better, I'd swear she'd suddenly turned into a guard dog.

My idea—to get away and hide—is going nowhere fast. And the fact that it takes me so long to get anywhere hobbling around on three legs isn't helping any. She spots me before I've barely gotten across the Dog Park.

With Angel coaxing Hattie to play with the Nanatoys, I was hoping she'd be preoccupied so I could make a quick getaway. But no such luck. Every time I try to ditch her, she's right on my tail. Of course I have no idea where I would go, but I have to find some peace. If only for a little while!

I'm beginning to think I'll have to put up with her bad surprises forever when I hear the jingling of dog tags from the other side of the fence. My tail shoots up with hope. I can always count on the ladies. Maybe they'll help with my plan.

I limp over to the side fence. "'Sup, ladies?"

Through a gap, I see Goldie trot over. Patches finishes a scratch, then does the same. "This separation is getting old," Goldie gruffs.

Patches sighs. "How are you holding up, Fenway?" she asks in her lovely voice. "It looks like those episodes in the wading pool have been rather hard on you."

"You can say that again. Between that and everything else, I can't take it anymore!"

Patches cocks her head. "It doesn't seem like there's much you can do."

Goldie snaps at a fly. "Yeah. Putting up a fight doesn't seem to be working for you."

"That's the problem," I say. "I've tried to get her to stop. I've tried to protect myself. But nothing has worked. I have no other choice. I have to get away for a while!"

The ladies gasp. "Fenway, you're not serious!" Patches cries.

Goldie's eyes bulge. "I hate to agree, but you two have always been so tight."

"I know," I say, sinking into the grass. "But I'm going nuts! I can't take even one more bath."

The ladies stare at me with sad eyes. "I guess wanting to hide out for a bit is understandable," Patches says.

"Hiding's a perfectly acceptable technique for dealing with problems," Goldie agrees. "Dogs do it all the time."

I glance back at the porch. Hattie's tapping the little clear box with the abracadabra stick again. And also gazing back at me. I turn to the ladies. "The problem is she knows all my moves," I say. "The second I slink off somewhere, she's on me. Plus, there aren't that many places to go."

"That's a problem all right," Patches says, full of empathy.

"But not an unsolvable one," Goldie chimes in. "You're small. You can squeeze into all kinds of spots."

"Or maybe an Opportunity will present itself," Patches offers.

Or maybe it won't. I shiver. I think about the pool-baths, the yucky-tasting cream, the pebbly morsels. "Thanks, ladies," I say. "I hope you're right."

For the rest of the day, I watch Hattie. And think.

I need two things—Opportunity and Destination. The bad news is I'm having trouble with both.

Patches said an Opportunity might present itself. The trouble is, how long will I have to wait?

While Hattie and Angel play on the porch, Hattie spends just as much time looking at me as she does the Nana-toys.

Finally, Hattie slams the abracadabra stick down in frustration and Angel goes home. As we head inside for supper, I get an idea. Maybe I've been going about this the wrong way. Maybe what I need to focus on isn't the Opportunity. Maybe it's the Destination.

We gather in the Eating Place like always, the wondrous aroma of pepperoni pizza tantalizing my nose.

Sitting beside Hattie's chair is exactly where she expects me to be. What I need is someplace that's the exact opposite.

But that's easier said than done. My mouth is watering and my tummy is rumbling. Maybe I should wait until after supper. Those pizza crusts and my tasty food are definitely worth waiting for!

When my belly is full and Hattie carries me upstairs, I still haven't spotted a Destination. We head down the hall and duck into the Bathtub Room. Hattie squeezes the little tube and squirts the yucky-tasting goo onto my white paw. I don't put up a fight. I'm biding my time.

While she puts the tube away, I hobble into her room and curl up under the chair. A moment later, she pokes her head through the door. "Come on, Fenway," she calls.

I don't move. I try to look as cozy as possible. With a

great big yawn, I close my eyes. Apparently, Hattie gives up. Her footsteps pad through the hallway and down the stairs.

My eyelids pop open. The coast is clear.

I gingerly get up. I need a Destination. Fetch Man and Food Lady's room? Nah. They'd find me and shoo me out . . . the Bathtub Room? Nah. Everybody goes in there. Plus, they'd probably plop me in the tub! I continue slinking down the hall. There's one door left. A place with terrible memories of being trapped behind The Gate and Hattie mad at me. The sharp paint smell has faded. It's been ages since I've gone inside . . .

I limp closer to the Destination, and good news— the door's not closed all the way. My snout wedges it open, just wide enough so I can sneak through. When I get inside, I nose it shut. Then I turn around.

Whoa. The empty room is not empty anymore! How did this happen?

I sniff my way over to a big bed and a small table. My nose buried in the shaggy white rug, I check out a dresser against the other wall. Wowee! There's so much stuff in this room, I hardly know where to focus.

I trot over to the same old windows I remember, except now there are long drapes on either side. Fetch Man's wooden ladder is beside the window on the back wall. There's a coffee mug and a hammer on top.

Is this that same horrible room? It looks completely different!

And it smells completely different, too. Instead of boring smells of dust and loneliness, I smell scents of paint and Food Lady and Fetch Man. And strangers, too. Those tall humans who came on the Evil Truck? I must gather more information!

I sniff every inch of the used-to-be-empty room. The scents certainly are curious. This place looks like a bedroom, but it doesn't smell like one at all. For starters, the bed smells like nobody's ever slept in it. The dresser smells like there's nothing inside it. The ladder smells like coffee, but it also smells like Fetch Man's tools and dirty work boots. Those are supposed to be in the garage, not inside the house!

Nose back to the floor, I resume sniff patrol. The fading paint smell is strongest on the walls. They're a bit darker than they were before, too. When did that happen?

As I'm scouting along the back wall, I hear a noise floating through the window and I stop mid-sniff. A horrible sound. Coming from the Dog Park.

Chip-chip-chip! Chip-chip-chip!

I know those sounds—it's that thieving chipmunk! What horrible crime is he committing in the Dog Park while nobody's there to stop him?

The sounds are moving closer, right underneath the window. Uh-oh! That means he's casing the porch! I leap and leap. I manage to scrape my claws on the wall, but I can't reach the sill. I jump higher and higher, my hind paws kicking wildly and—*whoa—oh—oooooh!*

The ladder is teetering and tilting. And . . . *scraaaaatch!* It knocks into the side wall. The mug and hammer go flying. *Bang! Thump!* Coffee sprays and splatters—*splash!*

And then—*thud!*—the ladder crashes into the bedside table. The lamp topples over and—*smash!* It smacks onto the floor.

Chapter 18

YIKES! This place sure got messy in a hurry!

And smelly! The aroma of stale coffee is everywhere—on the bed, on the rug, and even on the walls. I hop over to check it out.

Beside the bed, Fetch Man's coffee cup is on the floor. And the ladder is on its side—two legs on the floor and two in the air. Instead of being way-up-high, the top of the ladder is leaning on the bedside table. It's supposed to be standing up!

I look at the wall. A second ago, it was perfectly smooth. But now there's a big, long scrape. And a hole above the pillow, where Fetch Man's hammer is resting.

Talk about a big change! What else has happened?

My nose to the ground, I explore the rest of the room. Right away, I come across dark splotches all over the shaggy white rug. And shards of broken glass scattered around a lopsided lamp on the floor.

I'm steering clear of the pointy glass when my ears pick up sounds that make me stop in my tracks. Footsteps are thumping up the stairs!

Uh-oh. Somebody's coming.

I'm halfway to the bed when I hear the door being flung open. And Food Lady's gasp.

Fetch Man's, too. "What the—*Fenway!*" he shouts. His footsteps rush toward the bed. As I'm diving underneath, fingers brush against my tail.

I shoot out of Fetch Man's grasp. Ah, safety! Plus, the rug under the bed smells new and clean and not at all like stale coffee.

"Oh no!" Food Lady yells in her freak-out voice—her tone that's loud and upset and layered with panic. And usually followed by punishments.

Fetch Man sounds pretty upset himself. "FEN-way," he snaps. His sideways head appears on the floor. His arm reaches under the bed.

I creep toward the center of the bed. It's pretty obvious that nothing good would happen if I let him catch me.

"Oooh!" Food Lady cries. I hear her feet hurry to the wall behind the bed. Where that hole is. And the big scrape. "What—?! How?"

Fetch Man sighs. His arm withdraws and his face disappears. Apparently, he's given up on me.

His footsteps dash around the bed and join Food Lady. The two of them are chatting at the same time, their voices frantic and angry and sighing a lot. Also, kind of growly.

I hear Fetch Man go to the back window. "Hattie!" he calls.

I shiver at this development. Hattie's probably going to come inside and be angry right along with Fetch Man and Food Lady.

I stay put, right in the center of the space under the bed. Hattie won't be able to reach me. And there's no way she can coax me out, not even with a whole plate full of bacon. Or barbecued chicken!

I will stay here by myself no matter what. Eventually, the humans will have no choice but to give up and leave me alone.

I hear a series of creaks and then a soft thud, like the stepladder is getting put straight again. Probably by Fetch Man. Then I hear a rubbing sound on the wall. Is he patting it?

Food Lady moans. I see her feet on the far side of the bed. Her fingers pluck shards of glass out of the shaggy white rug.

Next thing I know, Hattie's footsteps pad up the stairs. She rushes into the room, gasping. "Oh no!" she cries. "How—?"

"Fenway," Food Lady says.

I hear murmuring and rumbling and scuttling. Then Hattie's bushy hair and sideways face peer under the bed. "Fenway, come," she says in a growly voice.

I curl into a ball, avoiding her gaze. What is she thinking? That I'll just come scampering out and let her be mad at me up close and personal? She's not even holding a treat.

"Hattie," Fetch Man mutters. Her face vanishes.

Have I won this round? I lie still and listen.

After a bunch of bossy chattering at Fetch Man and Hattie, Food Lady leaves the room. Fetch Man's footsteps sound behind her.

Above me—*whuuuuup! Thwuuuuup!* It sounds like blankets and sheets being pulled off. Hattie's feet walk around the bed.

Food Lady's footsteps return, along with clunky noises. Uh-oh. I get a terrible feeling. My body quakes. I curl up even tighter.

VREEEEE! VREEEEE!

YOWZA! It's that scary creature I know all too well—the tall, roaring Carpet Sucker!

VREEEEE! VREEEEE! Clat-clat-clat!

EEEEE-YOW! Its low mouth is screaming! It's clattering even more than usual! What's going on?

I creep to the edge of the bed, my snout poking into the room. Food Lady pushes that loud Carpet Sucker back and forth over the rug, her face grim with determination. Or anger. Either way, it's bad news.

I think about hobbling away, but where would I go? As soon as I'd head for the door, Hattie would probably grab me. And continue her horrible acts of torture!

If I have to stay put, at least I can try to make the Carpet Sucker stop. "Go away!" I bark, baring my teeth. "Take your loud clatter someplace else!"

But as usual, it doesn't listen. It keeps up that racket. *VREEEEE! Clat-clat-clat! Clat-clat-clat! Clat-clat-clat!*

Whoa. That's a lot of noisy glass being consumed. Food Lady's face is serious and frowning, her eyes focused on the rug. She keeps pushing that monster over the same spots again and again.

How much barking does it take to get that thing to be quiet? Apparently, quite a lot. "Beat it! Scram! Take your horrible sounds someplace else!" I don't stop barking until at long last, the Carpet Sucker goes quiet. Whew! My hard work finally paid off.

Right then, I hear Fetch Man's feet thudding up the stairs and striding into the room. He heads for the wall behind the bed. The one with the hole and big gash.

Food Lady pushes the now-quiet Carpet Sucker out of the room.

Fetch Man groans. With a *plunk!* his clunky toolbox lands on one of the ladder's steps. I edge out for a better look.

He grabs a small container that looks like a yogurt cup. My tail starts to wag. Whoopee! I love yogurt!

But when he rips off the lid, my tail abruptly stops. That container does not smell creamy and tangy like yogurt. It smells terrible, like paste. Or chalk.

Fetch Man takes a wide knife and smears the wet, chalky paste over the hole in the wall. He scrapes it smooth until the hole disappears. He does the same for the long gash. That yucky, pasty wet chalk odor is getting stronger. Pee-yew!

And that's not the only bad smell. When Food Lady returns, she plops down on her knees beside the dark splotches on the rug. She points a bottle and out comes—*eeeee-yowza!* A sharp, strong spray! It's piercing my nose! I crawl all the way back under the bed.

The humans keep working, their voices grumbling. Hattie comes in and out of the room a bunch of times, like she can't decide if she wants to stay or not. At first,

I think she's planning to play another trick on me. But every time I peek out, I only see her handing Food Lady more rags or Fetch Man more coffee. And she sounds just as hassled as they do. What's up with that? What's everybody so grumpy about?

The humans come and go and grunt as the windows grow darker and darker and darker. When they've finally turned to black, Hattie returns with a great big yawn. I hear her spreading the sheets and blankets on the bed above me.

The hiding spot's worked out pretty well, except for one thing. And I don't have to creep back to the edge of the bed to know what it is. *Yow-wee!* Wet paint!

Before I can think things through, I scoot out from under the bed. I have to escape that horrible smell!

"Fenway!" Hattie snaps. And her hands close around me.

Chapter 19

"Put me down!" I bark, wiggling like crazy. I know it won't do any good, but for some reason I have to try. "I won't put up with this!"

"FEN-way," Hattie growls. She rattles on and on in a scolding voice. What is she so mad about? I'm the one who got captured!

Hattie carries me downstairs, and we step outside for the shortest pee-stop ever. The abundance of teeny lights in the sky tells me it's way past bedtime. Normally, I'd be wondering why we're up so late, but this time it's pretty obvious. More tricks are coming!

How did this happen? I had the perfect plan to hide from her. And it was going great! I was out of sight, safely away from Hattie and all that torment. That is, until the tall humans came and ruined everything.

How did they find me so fast? I was so sure the used-to-be-empty room is the last place they'd look. Was it just bad luck they picked tonight to work on a big job in there? And Hattie, too?

Now Hattie's nabbed me and there's no place to hide. My tummy seizes with fear. I'm officially trapped.

I have no defense as Hattie plies me with yucky pills. Or when she dunks my paw in salty water and smears that horrible cream on my paw. She doesn't care that I'm miserable. She doesn't care that I'm desperate. She doesn't put me down until we get to her room. And she closes the door.

I head to my now-usual spot under the chair and keep an eye on her.

Hattie flops into bed, and I sigh with sadness. Bedtime used to be so happy—cozy blankets, snuggles and fur brushing, singing "best buddies." Yawning loudly, she touches the wall, and the room goes dark.

I cower under the chair, watching and waiting. A cool breeze drifts through the window screen. Crickets chirp. An owl hoots. I listen to Hattie's deep breathing—even and steady. She may be asleep. But for how long? She could wake up at any moment and get me.

I won't close my eyes all night long. I have to watch Hattie. I can't take any more bad surprises! I'm just a little dog!

I have to stay on guard, even though my eyelids are getting droopy. I rest my head on the rug . . .

And we're riding in the car. Hattie's in her pajamas, staring out the window. Distracted!

It's my chance! I quickly hop to the floor and dive under the seat. She'll never look for me down here.

Next thing I know, she's got me by the tail. Hey!

"Gotcha!" she shouts, her voice triumphant. She pulls me out from under the seat and hoists me onto her lap. Trapped again.

Whoa. How did that not work? I need a better idea. I think so hard, I might be trembling.

The car stops, and the door is flung open. Hattie carries me to a familiar and scary place that smells like dogs and cats and bunnies. Fear and panic, too. Oh no! It's the vet's office!

Hattie marches us into a room that's filled with whimpering, moaning dogs—Poodles and Labs and Corgis and Golden Doodles and Chihuahuas and Pit Bulls. Each one of them is groaning and wailing. "I don't want to get poked!" one of them cries.

"No more sliding table!" whines another.

I begin to shake uncontrollably. I cannot do this again. While Hattie speaks to the lady behind the counter, I spy Opportunity.

I leap out of her arms and crawl around a chair. She'll never find me in this crowd.

On the table next to me, a cat is locked up in a cage. She's hissing and meowing. She sounds forceful and threatening. Chip-chip-chip! she calls.

Huh? My fur prickles. If I didn't know better, I'd say she sounds like that thieving chipmunk. What's happened to this cat?

"Aha!" Hattie shouts. Her fingers reach behind the chair.

Oh no! I scramble to get to the other side. "I won't let you—" I start to bark.

But it's no use. She's grabbed me. Before I know it, she whisks us into another room that's tiny and cold. There's a metal table with no legs. It sounds like chirping crickets and hooting owls. And it reeks of terror and wet paint!

"No! No, Hattie!" I wail. "Please let's go someplace else. Anywhere but heeeeere!" I wiggle and squirm, but she's holding me tight. There's no escape!

Hattie's pajamas turn into a white coat. Her bushy hair wraps up into a loose pile on top of her head. She smells spicy, like cinnamon.

As she reaches for a long, poke-y needle, her grip relaxes. Another Opportunity! I squirt out of her arms and drop to the floor. I fly under the Table of Panic. She'll never see me down here.

A soft breeze floats in from somewhere. And an annoying voice. Chip-chip-chip!

What?! Hattie sounds exactly like that thieving chipmunk, too. Are my ears playing tricks on me? I cock my head and listen some more.

Chip-chip-chip! *Hattie calls again. And what's that other noise she's making? It sounds like chewing or gnawing. Is she eating that scary needle? It doesn't smell like food . . .*

"Aha!" *she yells again. Her fingers clasp my collar and lift me up.*

Yikes! I gaze into her face, horrified. Her eyes are glowing with evil triumph. Is this my Hattie? What has happened to her?

She whips around, and my eyes nearly pop out of my head. Right in front of us is a great big plastic bathtub! And sniff . . . sniff . . . *It's filled with creamy goo that smells bitter!*

"No way!" *I yelp, twisting furiously as she lowers me into the goo. It's seeping into my fur . . . like water?*

THUD! *Did a chair just fall over?*

I can't see! I'm thrashing and paddling, and water and goo is sloshing all over the place. It's cold and wet. And my fur is completely soaked!

I'm sinking . . . down . . . down . . . down . . .

"Help me!" *I shriek, gasping for breath.* "Somebody help me! Please—?"

CHapteR 20

"Fenway?"

Is that Hattie's groggy voice? My eyes blink open. Warm sunlight streams into the room.

I'm sprawled on the floor, flanked by a toppled chair and Hattie's empty drinking cup. Half of my body is soaking wet.

A haunting reminder of the evil I've endured!

I get up and shake. Drops of water spray all around.

"FEN-way," Hattie snaps. She lifts off the covers, groaning, and climbs out of bed. She straightens the chair and returns the drinking cup to her bedside table. Wagging a finger at me, she says, "Bad boy!"

Talk about a mix-up! She's the one who did something

wrong! My ears and tail drooping, I back into the corner. What a way to start the day.

Sighing, Hattie glances around the room. She grabs the shirt she was wearing yesterday and rubs it on the rug, scowling at the wet spot like it's done something terrible to her.

I watch closely as she hangs the damp shirt on the back of the chair and pulls on her clothes. When she opens the door, she heads out, but I hold up. I could stay right where I am and be safe. But not for long.

She'd return eventually, and I'd be a sitting duck.

I need to do something. That last hiding place didn't work out so well. But I have to keep trying.

I hobble down the stairs and limp into the Lounging Place, my nose sniffing, my head swiveling. The only good hiding place in here is under the couch. And that spot has failed me before. I have to continue searching!

Food Lady and Fetch Man are already in the Eating Place, gulping steaming cups of coffee. Their eyes are saggy and tired. Fetch Man tries to stifle a yawn. Food Lady, too.

Hattie pours a glass of juice, her face just as grumpy and exhausted as theirs.

After Fetch Man swigs the last of his coffee, he ducks into the garage. He reappears with a light bulb and heads upstairs.

Food Lady chatters at Hattie, her voice harried and anxious. She says a word that I know. "Ready?"

Usually this word is followed by smiles and bouncing. Maybe even cries of excitement. From both of us. But this time, Hattie looks worried. Like she's not ready at all.

I know just how she feels.

And I can't waste my time trying to figure out what Hattie's not ready for. I've got my own job to do.

I could hide under the table, but how obvious is that? Same with the chairs. Too bad the low cabinets are closed. Plus they are filled with nasty things like cleaners.

Clearly, there are no good hiding spots in the Eating Place. Which is too bad, because there are a bunch of perks in here. Like food.

I briefly consider the boring room down the hall. But Fetch Man and Food Lady guard that place like it's filled with steaks. Even though there's nothing inside but a couple of desks and chairs with wheels on the bottom.

No, the best option for a good hiding place is the Dog Park. I limp to the door. "Let me out!" I whine. "I have to go sooooo bad!"

"FEN-way," Hattie scolds, like she's not falling for it. But she must change her mind, because she hurries over and slides the door open. *F-f-f-t!*

At least I can count on her for something. As I hobble outside, I hear the door close behind me. Aaaaah! I'm finally alone!

Right away I know something is wrong. I turn my snout into the breeze, gathering clues. The air smells strongly of rodent. And peanuts. My hackles shoot up. That thieving chipmunk was here! No doubt robbing us blind!

My head hangs. My ears flop. This can only mean one thing.

I didn't do my job. Drat that Cone of Doom! Drat my sore paw! Drat everything!

It's all my fault that that chipmunk roamed wherever he wanted, free to do his dirty work. All that's left to do now is survey the damage.

Nose to the floor, I sniff that horrible rodent-y scent. It smells like the chipmunk was all over the place. But the odor is weak, like he's already taken off.

I sniff my way past Hattie's old sneakers, under a couple of chairs, toward the Nana-box. And that's when I freeze.

The Nana-box is open. The cape, the tall hat, the abracadabra stick, and the other Nana-toys are strewn all over the porch. Hattie always stuffs them back inside the box when she's done playing. Why are they on the floor?

And if that's not strange enough, everything reeks of that thieving chipmunk. I shiver.

I limp over to investigate, but I'm not even halfway to the abracadabra stick when I stop. My eyes bulge.

That stick has been chewed.

Little teeth marks run up and down the stick. Tiny chunks are missing at one end.

I hobble up to the rumpled cape. I nose through the folds, my fur standing up in horror. The fabric is torn! It's been chewed just like the abracadabra stick!

And if that's not bad enough, everything's covered with bits of stinky dark rice—no, not rice! Chipmunk droppings! They're everywhere!

I search through the rest of the Nana-toys. The brim of the tall hat is gnawed and frayed. The wooden ball has tiny teeth marks and gashes in it. The clear plastic box has a crack in it. And the fake flowers are in tatters.

And there's more! The peanut bag is ripped, shreds littered around. Peanut shells are all over. And slimy bits of chewed peanuts speckle the porch like pebbles.

It's clear what's happened here—that villain didn't only rob us, he had a chipmunk party!

I shudder at the images of thieving chipmunks romping and munching right under my nose. Partying on the porch, like they own the place!

It's too scary to even picture. It's scarier than the Nana-box—Hey, wait a minute!

The Nana-box is the Best Hiding Place Ever.

I've told Hattie a million times how I feel about that box. She'd never look for me in there.

Gulp. Before I can talk myself out of it, I spring onto the chair. I peer down into the Nana-box. It's empty all right.

And with the lid up, it might not be so scary inside. Probably not anyway.

Trembling with courage, I drop down and land *splat!* inside the Nana-box.

And just in time.

CHAPTER 21

I hear Hattie's footsteps padding out onto the porch.

"Fenway?" she calls, sounding puzzled.

I curl up tight. The Nana-box smells old and musty. It's full of scary memories. But at least it's open and bright. Overhead, the sky is clear. Sunlight pours in and warms my back.

But there's still plenty to worry about. This box is a great place to hide as long as Hattie doesn't get too close to peek in.

"Fenway!" she calls again. Her feet scuffle across the porch and into the Dog Park. "Fenn-waay! Oh, Fenn-waay!"

I shiver. Clearly, she's searching for me. This cannot be good.

She's probably got more evil on her mind. Like pebbly morsels or yucky cream or—*gulp!*—the pool-bath! I've put up with her tricks long enough. I can't stand it anymore!

The sounds of her footsteps are getting fainter and fainter. I picture her at the back of the Dog Park and circling the giant tree, then roaming up the side fence and looking under the bushes. I hear her cross to the other side fence and imagine her scanning the vegetable patch. "Fenway?" she cries, rattling the Friend Gate. It sounds like it's shut tight.

I resist the urge to stretch up and peek out of the Nana-box. I can't risk her finding me. The stakes are too high!

Especially now . . . because I'm pretty sure I hear her rushing in this direction. "Fenway! Fenway!" she calls more urgently. She's starting to sound worried. She must be awfully desperate to return to her dastardly deeds!

I make myself as small and quiet as possible. One accidental noise and she could discover my hiding spot.

She pads up the porch steps, probably about to head into the house. Maybe she thinks I snuck back in there while she was distracted.

Her footsteps thud onto the porch and suddenly stop. She gasps.

Oh no! I shake with terror. Has she realized I'm hiding inside the Nana-box? Is she about to nab me?

I don't dare breathe. I expect to see her grabby hands at any moment. I can't bear to look.

But her hands do not appear. Instead, I hear more horrified gasps. "No! No!" she wails. She sprints around the porch, sounding panicked, crying, "No!" over and over, as if she's making one terrible discovery after another. Is she noticing the pooped-on cape and hat and chewed abracadabra stick? The stolen peanuts? The rest of the ruined Nana-toys?

Hattie stops, and I hear different noises. Little sobs. And sniffles.

F-f-f-f-t! The door slides open again. "Hattie?" Food Lady says.

"Look!" Hattie cries.

"What?!" Food Lady says in a surprised voice. She hurries across the porch, right toward me.

"How—?" Hattie begins, but right then another noise drowns out everything else.

BEEEEEP! BEEEEEP!

Out in the driveway, a car door slams. A trunk pops open. Is Fetch Man returning? Was he gone? I cock my head and listen, my hackles up. Are intruders coming?

161

In unison, Food Lady and Hattie gasp. "Nana!" they both cry.

Nana? I don't hear Nana. Could Nana be here?

"Quick!" Food Lady says, rushing around. *Whoosh! Clatter! Plunk!* What is she doing—

Hey! Suddenly, I'm buried under silky cloths. Soft toys pile on top of me. For an instant, I consider pulling them off. And then—

THUNK!

The lid clunks down. The Nana-box goes dark. Uh-oh! I'm trapped! I wiggle and kick. I have to get out of here!

Outside, I hear the muffled sounds of the screen door sliding open . . . Food Lady's and Hattie's footsteps racing through . . . *thud!* The door slams shut.

How can they leave at a time like this?

I must find a way to escape. I'm clearly on my own. If only it weren't so cramped and crowded in here!

I rustle through folds of cloth, wriggling and climbing. My nose tells me I'm wrapped in Hattie's cape. I paw and squirm and wiggle until finally my head pokes out—but I'm not free.

I'm buried!

Whoa. There's a lot more stuff in here than I thought! More sniffs confirm that the tall hat, the abracadabra stick, and most of the other Nana-toys are all around me. They shift and fall whenever I move. And they all reek of rodent and *sniff . . . sniff . . .* something else . . .

Ewwwww! Stinky chipmunk droppings! A horrendous reminder of how I've failed.

I couldn't keep the Dog Park safe, and now I'm paying the price.

I bend and kick and swipe. Toys tumble and drop, some falling on either side of me while others hover overhead. I'm surrounded by obstacles. There's barely enough room in here to move. Or breathe!

My hind paw skids on something hard and round—the wooden ball! My front paw catches in something—a metal ring!

No matter how I twist or where I turn, Nana-toys are in my way. I can't make any progress at all!

And everywhere I look, it's so DARK!

I sniff every corner, searching for a way out. But I don't find one. There's absolutely no hope!

But I can't give up. I claw the fake flowers out of my face. I swat the tall hat to one side. I bite a silky scarf that's wound around my paw. *R-r-r-rip!*

I climb on toy after toy. At last, I can stretch up high enough to reach the lid. I push against it with my snout. "Open up, you scary Nana-box!" I growl.

I shove and shove with all my might. But the lid doesn't budge one single bit. It is shut tight.

I sink back down with a horrifying realization—I might be trapped in here forever.

I collapse into a heap of surrender. There's no escape from the Nana-box.

Unless I can come up with an idea. A really good idea.

I can't open this lid. And I'm pretty sure it won't open all by itself. When I was trapped before, I barked and yelped and made lots of noise until Hattie came and let me out. It was a lot of hard work. But it got the job done.

When it comes to hard work, I'm a professional. But what would happen this time? If Hattie opened the Nana-box right now, would I leap into her loving arms? Or would she leave me where I am?

I tremble. Do I want to get out of this scary Nana-box enough to risk being tortured again? Is it too much to hope that Hattie would change back to the loving and fun self that she was before?

I'm shaking and fidgeting and thinking so hard, I'm barely aware of noises outside. Humans chattering. Hattie . . . Food Lady and Fetch Man . . . and somebody else . . . Nana?

They all sound alarmed. What's that about?

Plop! Somebody sinks into the chair right beside me. Hattie? She sniffles. She sobs. She's obviously sad and miserable.

Gulp.

Clearly, she feels bad that the thieving chipmunk stole her peanuts and ruined her toys. She spent so much time playing with them. And now they are wrecked. I knew that rodent was trouble. If only I could've stopped him. If only I could've protected Hattie's things from danger.

Gulp. Gulp.

Hattie tries to speak, her voice catching. She sounds more upset than ever. "Fenway," she croaks over and over. She knows I'm to blame. She knows I've let her down. If only I could've prevented this senseless attack.

My heart is breaking. Maybe my paw was sore and I couldn't run. Maybe Hattie turned against me. But there's still no excuse for not doing my job. And now she's crushed, and it's all my fault.

What kind of dog am I?

@Hapter 22

Hattie turned on me. She handed me over to Spicy Breath. She tormented me with the pool-bath and the creamy goo. She forced pebbly morsels down my throat. I'm hiding because it hurt too much to be with her.

But it hurts way more to be without her.

She's my short human. We mean everything to each other.

And now she's miserable. She's sobbing. She's choke-breathing. "F-f-f-fen-waaaaay," she wails, her voice broken.

Am I the kind of dog who throws in the towel when the going gets tough?

Not when it comes to loving my Hattie. Especially now when she's sad and she needs me.

Maybe she's up to no good. Maybe she played tricks. But she's still Hattie, and it's my job to make her happy again. Nothing has ever been more important!

I take a deep breath. I point my snout toward the top of the Nana-box. Giving it all I've got, I bark into the darkness. "I'm here! I'm here, Hattie! I'm right here!"

I pause and listen.

But Hattie keeps on crying. Either she doesn't hear, or she can't recognize the sound of her own loyal dog.

I paw and push and bump the Nana-box as hard as I can. I claw and thump. I have to show her that I'm here. I have to get her to rescue me.

Right then, I get the Best Idea Ever. I take another deep breath, and howl at the top of my lungs. "Best buddies, best buddies . . ."

I cock my head.

Has she stopped crying? Is that her voice murmuring?

I listen harder.

"F-f-f-fen-waaaaay?"

I'd know that sweet voice anywhere—it's my Hattie!

"Best buddies, best buddies . . ." I howl some more.

I pause and listen again.

Rustling sounds. Fidgeting. Creaking. Is the Nana-box opening?

I squint into the light. Bright sky is overhead. Brilliant sun. And Hattie's glowing face!

I shake and bounce. "Hattie! Hattie!"

Her hands reach in and lift me up. "Fenway! Fenway!" she cries.

I snuggle her wet, salty cheek. She strokes my back. My tail goes nuts. "I'm ready to make you happy again!" I bark.

Hattie smiles. She hugs me close. We sway back and forth.

I sigh with gladness. Wrapped in Hattie's arms is the Best Place to Be.

She sets me down, and I romp in circles. I zip around the porch, over Food Lady's sandals, in front of Fetch Man's sneakers, because up ahead is . . . Nana!

Sniff . . . sniff . . . Oooooh, she smells just as wonderful as before! Licorice and coffee and *mmmmm* exactly the right amount of cherry. Nana! "I'm so happy to see you!" I leap on her legs, my tail on over-swish.

Nana scootches down. I gaze into her eyes that crinkle on the outside and sparkle on the inside. Her long hair hangs over one shoulder, dark and silvery. We rub noses. "Aw, Fenway," she coos.

I lick her face. I love Nana!

"Aw . . ." Hattie giggles.

I race over to her. "I love you, too, Hattie!"

Fetch Man and Food Lady laugh and clap. I fly over to them, then gallop back to Hattie again. I'm so happy! I can't control myself!

And neither can the humans. They are grinning and cheering and reaching out to pet me, like having me back is the greatest thing that's ever happened.

What can I say?

It's such a wonderful moment, all I can do is leap and spin. And jump on Hattie. And paw her legs . . . Hey! My white paw doesn't hurt or itch anymore. And it's not puffy, either.

Wowee! I zip across the porch. Hooray! I can prance and run and do whatever I want!

My paw is back to normal! And it's perfectly obvious how it happened.

Hattie did it! I knew I could count on her when I needed her most. Maybe she tortured me. And played tricks on me. But she still loves me. When I was at my most desperate, she rescued me, and that made everything all better.

I throw myself at her. "Hooray! Hooray!" I bark, snuggling her ankles. "You're a hero!"

She gathers me into her arms again. "Aw, Fenway," she sings.

"I never doubted you for one single second," I bark,

twisting my head for more ear scratches. "Oh, yeah. That's the spot. Right there."

When she puts me down, I romp some more. Whoopee! It sure feels great to be able to use my white paw again.

Fetch Man puts his arm around Food Lady. She looks relieved.

Nana heads for the Nana-box, like she's just noticed it's there.

Hattie beats her to it. She fishes out the ruined cape, the chewed hat, the gnawed abracadabra stick. She turns to Nana and frowns. "No-show," she says, her voice dripping with disappointment.

Nana gazes at Hattie with her crinkly, sparkly eyes. She pulls Hattie into a hug. "It's okay," Nana soothes.

Hattie grumbles, "Hattie-the-Grrate . . ."

Nana turns toward me, gesturing dramatically. I feel their stares as I scamper around. Nana points at Hattie's chest. "Hattie-the-Grrate!" she says.

Hattie buries her face in Nana's shoulder. She smells happy. "Aw, Nana," she murmurs.

Nana strokes Hattie's bushy hair, full of approval. She must be really appreciating that hug because that's all Hattie's doing, and Nana's acting totally impressed.

"Hey, I like hugs, too!" I bark, nudging my way between them.

Hattie scoops me up and rocks me from side to side. Me and Hattie are together and loving each other, and Nana is here. We're having so much fun, I begin to think it can't get any better. Until the Friend Gate swings open.

My tail thumps. Yippee! Our friends are coming.

I spring out of Hattie's arms and rush into the Dog Park. Hattie's right behind me.

Angel bursts through the gate. Hattie greets her with whoops of excitement. "Fenway!" she says to Angel. "Look!" She points at me, even though I'm leaping on Angel's legs and there's no way she could possibly not notice me.

Angel's face lights up with surprise. And admiration. She reaches down and gently strokes my white paw. "Aw, Fenway," she coos.

I'm not sure what she was expecting. But it's sure nice to be appreciated for just being myself. I lick her hand. "Thanks!"

Hattie continues chattering, full of pride and happiness. Angel pulls the Friend Gate open again and calls for . . . the ladies!

Wowee! I jump and twirl. Goldie and Patches are loping through the gate. Hooray! Hooray! My friends are back!

"You were gone for such a long time, ladies," I say,

racing up for some long overdue sniff-greetings. "I'm so glad you're back!"

Goldie noses me playfully. "We are, too."

"Fenway!" Patches cries, her eyes wide and bright. "You're back to your old self!"

I wave my white paw in the air, my tail swaying with pride. "It's all better!" I say. "Hattie's love for me healed it!"

Goldie and Patches exchange surprised looks. "Really?" Goldie says.

Patches gives her a nudge. "That's wonderful, Fenway."

"And guess what else?" I say, circling my friends. "Nana's here!"

The ladies turn toward the porch. Hattie and Angel are smiling and chatting with Nana while Fetch Man and Food Lady look on proudly. Nana cups her hand over Angel's ear and pulls out a shiny coin. The short humans gasp with delight, their faces beaming.

"Even from over here, I can tell Nana's a lot of fun," Goldie says.

Patches nods. "I have to agree. Nana appears downright lovable, like a member of the family."

I gaze at Nana. Hattie and Angel can't stop giggling. "Nana's exactly like a member of the family."

Goldie snatches a stick. She bows low on her fore-paws, her bum up high. She wants to play!

Me and Patches tear after her, racing around the Dog Park. Our tongues are lolling. Our sides are heaving. We're playing again like always, and it's the Most Fun Ever!

Goldie rounds the giant tree. She turns to us, waggling the stick. It's the very definition of irresistible!

"That stick is mine!" I call, sprinting up to Goldie. Patches is right on my tail.

Goldie taunts us with it, a devilish gleam in her eye. She takes off, and we chase her toward the bushes. We're almost there when I hear a fur-tingling sound.

Chip-chip-chip!

I stop in my tracks, looking around.

Under the bushes, a chipmunk head pops out—No! Lots of chipmunk heads! Am I seeing things? Or has that thieving chipmunk multiplied?

One is bigger than the others. *Chip-chip-chip!* it chirps. The smaller ones are making noises, too. *Squeak! Squeak! Squeak!*

My fur rises in protest. "Go away, you thieving chipmunk!" I bark. "You've stolen your last peanut!"

"Not so fast, Fenway," Patches says, following my gaze. "They probably have a home under there."

"I'll bet the whole chipmunk family's crammed into

a tiny hole under those bushes," Goldie says, suddenly the chipmunk expert.

As I creep closer, I see she's right. One by one, the small chipmunks disappear into the same spot in the ground. The biggest one—the mama?—is the last to vanish.

I crawl under the lowest branch and notice something else. Shreds of silky black fabric . . . tangled strings . . . bits of peanut shell . . .

I knew it!

"Those things are Hattie's, not yours!" I bark at the tiny hole. "You'll never get away with this!"

Hattie's probably just as concerned as I am because she and Angel dash over. Dropping onto their bellies, they shimmy under the bushes. They approach the hole so cautiously, they're not even breathing. Like they're approaching a flaming-hot barbecue.

"Fenway," Hattie whispers, shooing me out of the way.

What's the big deal? I've never seen short humans so alarmed by a bunch of rodents. Have they finally realized how treacherous they are?

I creep up to Hattie's shoulder. She and Angel peer into the tiny hole. "Awwwww," Angel says, pointing.

Hattie obviously spies her missing stuff. Her eyes get big. "Aha!" she says.

I scrape the ground with my two strong paws. "Consider yourselves on notice, chipmunk family!" I bark. "I'm back on the job!"

"Fenway," Hattie says, tucking me under her arm and patting my head. Clearly, she's grateful. Not to mention reassured.

Later, my whole family is gathered around the table. Now that I'm back in business, I'm hungrier than ever. I perch between Hattie's and Nana's chairs, smacking my chops.

The Eating Place is filled with the mind-blowing aroma of barbecued chicken and buttery potatoes. And the tired-kind-of-happiness that comes from a wonderfully busy day.

Food Lady and Fetch Man had ushered Nana through the entire house—even the boring room and the musty-smelling place. As Nana oohed and aahed at everything like she'd never been inside a house before, they both grinned proudly. As if they'd done a big job that was totally worth it.

When Hattie showed off her own room, Nana gasped and gushed as if it was the greatest place she'd ever seen. And then, something amazing happened—the used-to-be bear suddenly reappeared! Nana reached under Hattie's blankets and, without a word, pulled him right out! She hugged him tight like she'd been missing him, too.

Finally, we all checked out the used-to-be-empty room. It was once again neat and clean, until Fetch Man brought all of Nana's bags and cases inside. After that, it turned into an explosion of clothes and books and even a bunch of new toys for Hattie and me!

We sat on the bed while Nana played with the used-to-be bear. A needle and thread, too. When she was done, both of his button eyes were back!

Hattie gave Nana a hug and tossed him to me— *chomp!* I circled the room once before I let Hattie catch me. Game over!

"Best buddies, best buddies," she sang.

I raised my head and joined in. "Best buddies, best buddies," I howled.

"Wow!" Nana cried, clearly astonished. She clapped and clapped and clapped.

Hattie smiled proudly, cradling me in her arms. And then, we both took a bow.

Acknowledgments

For a Long, Long Time, I've wondered what dogs must think when we try to give them medicine. One day, I invited my neighbor Megan Brandwein, a veterinarian, to come over and talk about it. To my delight, she was not only willing to help brainstorm what can go wrong when a dog is hard to treat, but she was also full of anecdotes about caring for rambunctious Jack Russell terriers. Turns out, they are not the best patients.

And it also turns out that my own dog Kipper could give those JRTs a run for their money. He is such a bad patient that it takes at least two of us to take him to the vet—and that's when we can actually get him in the door (one time the vet had to give him his shots in an alley). So the good news is I had plenty of inspiration. Thank you, Kipper!

Huge thanks to my (former) neighbor Megan (whose

resemblance to Spicy Breath is not a coincidence) and my brilliant goddaughter Daniela Yuschenkoff, soon-to-be DVM. Without these ladies' expert help, advice, and fact-checking, I could not have written this story. Here's hoping none of their future patients are as hard to handle as Fenway!

Even with all that inspiration and access to medical info, creating a book is a lot trickier than waving a wand. I feel incredibly lucky for the chance to work with the world's greatest editor, Susan Kochan. Her insight, guidance, and amazing support are beyond anything I could wish for. There are not enough thanks to express how grateful I feel to be able to learn from her.

Penguin Young Readers is full of amazing people who perform feats of magic every day. I am in awe of and thankful to Amalia Frick, Dave Kopka, and Alexis Watts, to name just a few of the unsung heroes who lend their talents to creating and marketing my books.

If I could say *abracadabra* and make the ideal literary agent appear, she would be Marietta Zacker. No author could possibly be in better hands than with this dynamic, sharp, and caring lady. Endless thanks to Marietta, Erin Casey, and the whole team at Gallt & Zacker, who are total pros and even better people.

A spot-on manuscript critique is a pretty neat trick. Many thanks to my astute readers, critiquers, and friends Cheryl Lawton Malone, Cynthia Levinson, Theresa Milstein, Judy Mintz, Lisa J. Rogers, Pat Sherman, and Donna Woelki. If anything is more amazing than these ladies' helpful feedback, it's their generosity.

Hands down, my favorite part of being an author is connecting with readers. I am endlessly thankful to the wonderful champions whose boundless enthusiasm and talents have helped share my books with readers, especially John Schumacher, Margie Myers-Culver, Rachel Harder, Jason Lewis, Melissa Guerrette, Michele Knott, Dana Williams, Dalila Eckstein, Lesley Burnap, Julie Kirchner, Melanie Roy, Jana Eschner, Kurt Stroh, Carrie Davies, Jennifer Kelley Reed, Emily Montjoy, Corrina Allen, Biff Donovan, Bill Grace, Kathy Detwiler, Margie Leonard, Sara Grochowski, and Melissa Brilliant. Every one of these professionals has gone way above and beyond the call of duty to get the Fenway and Hattie books into the hands of readers. I am so, so grateful to them and every book champion out there. They are all heroes!

One of the biggest heroes is Pernille Ripp— teacher, author, speaker, and founder of the Global Read Aloud. I am beyond grateful and honored that Pernille chose *Fenway and Hattie* for the 2017 GRA, giving me the opportunity to connect with readers all over the world. Whenever I get to interact with readers is the Best Day Ever.

One of those Best Days was at the official launch of *Fenway and Hattie and the Evil Bunny Gang*. After I signed her books, Olivia Van Ledtje shot one of her famous #livbits videos with me, which began a magical connection that continues to wow me every day. This young lady is on a mission to make the world a better place by spreading the love of reading and empowering kids by promoting digital citizenship. I am honored to connect with and support this special reader! Please check out what she's up to at www.thelivbits.com. Go, Liv!

Speaking of support, I am forever in debt to Cheryl Lawton Malone, Bridget Hodder, and Elly Swartz, who teach me and encourage me on a daily basis. Lygia Day Peñaflor, Monica Tesler, Laura Shovan, and the rest of the Sweet Sixteens 2016 debut authors listen, cheer, celebrate, and offer guidance whenever I need it. I adore these authors as much as I love their books!

And finally, love and gigantic thanks to my family— Ralph, Philip, James, Mom, Dad, Walter, my brother and sister and their families, and all the Gormans and Wallaces. I hope I've made you proud.

Victoria J. Coe is a voracious reader, writing teacher, and Jack Russell terrier impersonator. She lives with her family on the outskirts of Boston, where she and her old dog are always learning new tricks.

www.victoriajcoe.com
instagram.com/victoriajcoe
Twitter: @victoriajcoe